SPEED TRAP

This Large Print Book carries the
Seal of Approval of N.A.V.H.

Speed Trap

Patricia Davids

THORNDIKE PRESS

A part of Gale, Cengage Learning

 GALE
CENGAGE Learning™

Detroit • New York • San Francisco • New Haven, Conn • Waterville, Maine • London

GALE
CENGAGE Learning

Copyright © 2009 by Patricia MacDonald.
Thorndike Press, a part of Gale, Cengage Learning.

LIBRARY OF CONGRESS CATALOGING-IN-PUBLICATION DATA

Davids, Patricia.
    Speed trap / by Patricia Davids.
      p. cm. — (Thorndike Press large print Christian mystery)
    ISBN-13: 978-1-4104-2966-7 (large print : hardcover)
    ISBN-10: 1-4104-2966-0 (large print : hardcover)
    1. Sheriffs—Fiction. 2. Policewomen—Fiction. 3. Family
violence—Fiction. 4. Large type books. I. Title.
PS3604.A9454S64 2010
813'.6—dc22   2010016592

Published in 2010 by arrangement with Harlequin Books S.A.

Printed in the United States of America
1 2 3 4 5 6 7 14 13 12 11 10

Therefore if any man be in Christ,
he is a new creature: old things are
passed away; behold, all things
have become new.

— *2 Corinthians* 5:17

To my brothers, all four of you,
for making me the toughest girl in
Navarre grade school. May God bless
and keep each one of you.

ONE

The black skid marks on the highway ended abruptly at a shattered guardrail. There was only empty space beyond.

Sheriff Mandy Scott maneuvered her white SUV to a stop before the break and mentally prepared herself for what lay over the edge.

It wouldn't be good.

Someone had found one of the worst spots in Morrison County to run his or her car off the road.

Mandy silenced her siren but left the light bar flashing. Grasping the radio mic, she reported in. "Dispatch, I'm on the scene."

Donna Clareborn, the county dispatcher, replied, "Copy that, Sheriff. Was Mr. Tobin right? Is there a fatality?"

"I don't know yet."

The accident had been called in by an elderly local rancher. Mandy saw his green pickup truck sitting a dozen yards down the highway, but Emmett was nowhere in sight.

"Fire rescue and EMS are on the way." A slight quiver in Donna's normally professional voice revealed her apprehension.

Mandy felt the same way. In a small community like Timber Wells, the victim could easily be someone they knew.

Grabbing her first-aid kit and fire extinguisher, Mandy left her vehicle. The early morning wind greeted her with the fresh scent of prairie grass and spring wildflowers before the stench of burning oil overpowered it. Mandy looked over the broken railing into the ravine.

Thirty feet below, a crumpled red car rested upside down in the dry creek bed. Spirals of gray smoke rose from the mangled front end.

Emmett Tobin sat in the grass a few feet from the vehicle. His gray head was bowed, his shoulders slumped. He held his sweat-stained Stetson between his hands.

Mandy sucked in a steadying breath, then made her way down the steep rocky slope.

Emmett looked up at her approach. "She's gone, Sheriff. There weren't nothing I could do."

Mandy laid a comforting hand on his shoulder. "You stayed with her, Emmett. That's something. I'll take it from here."

She didn't doubt his findings, but she had to check for herself. Leaving him, she approached the car. The air near the vehicle reeked of gasoline, burned rubber and hot oil. She cast a worried glance at the smoke curling out of the engine block.

Moving around the car, Mandy found the driver's side door had been flung open. A woman with short blond hair lay sprawled on her back beside it. She wore jeans and a bloodstained yellow shirt.

Kneeling beside the body, Mandy checked for a pulse and found none.

"Sheriff, you'd better get away from that car," Emmett called out sharply.

Mandy glanced up to see the smoke from the engine had become a thick black column with flames flickering at the base. It was then she heard a whimper — a tiny cry almost lost in the wind.

Was there someone still inside?

Mandy aimed her extinguisher at the burning engine. "Emmett, I need your help!"

Hurrying to her side, Emmett accepted the red canister Mandy thrust at him. Leaving him to deal with the flames, she knelt and peered inside the crushed vehicle. All she saw was a wadded-up blanket behind the passenger's seat, but she heard another muffled cry.

The driver's body was blocking Mandy's way. Slipping her hands under the woman's arms, Mandy dragged the body a few feet away. She could hear sirens now. The fire truck was almost here.

Emmett continued aiming bursts of CO_2 at the engine. The flames leaped higher. One extinguisher wouldn't be enough. The whole car could go up any second.

Breathing a quick prayer, Mandy ducked inside and began wiggling across the ceiling of the upside-down vehicle.

"Sheriff, what are you doing?" Emmett yelled. "I looked in. I didn't see nobody else."

"I hear crying. It sounds like a baby."

Broken glass covered everything. It bit into Mandy's elbows and stomach as she crawled. She could feel the heat of the fire. Smoke stung her eyes and scorched her lungs with each breath she was forced to take.

Behind the passenger's seat, she pushed aside a patchwork quilt and discovered a baby buckled into a car seat that had come loose. The child whimpered pitifully.

"You need to get out of there," Emmett shouted.

Barely able to move in the tight space,

Mandy worked frantically to unbuckle the remaining straps holding the child in the seat. Fear made her fingers clumsy.

Don't think about the fire. Get this child out.

The hiss and pop of the flames grew louder. The metal in the roof supports groaned as the weight of the car compressed them. If they crumpled a few more inches she would be trapped.

Tugging again at the fastener, she wished she had a knife, anything to cut the nylon straps.

God, please let me save this child.

Finally, the reluctant buckle clicked open. As Mandy pulled the baby loose, he cried out in pain.

"I'm sorry," she whispered, swaddling the blanket over him to protect him from the smoke. Cradling him close, she began to wiggle backward.

The heat of the engine fire singed her face and neck. She knew the smell of scorched cotton was coming from her uniform. With a loud metallic snap, the car settled lower.

The baby stopped crying, but she didn't dare unwrap him to see if he was okay. They were almost out of time.

"Please, God, only a little bit more."

She had her legs out when suddenly she felt hands grabbing her boots. An instant later, someone was pulling her free.

Emmett, having abandoned the empty extinguisher, helped her to her feet. They both turned and ran. With a deafening boom, the gas tank exploded and the flames engulfed the vehicle.

When they reached a safe distance, Mandy sank to her knees in the grass and stared at the blazing car.

"That was a near thing," Emmett wheezed beside her, bracing his hands on his knees.

"Much too close."

She looked down at the child she held and uncovered his face. To her relief he was still breathing. She sent a silent prayer of thanks.

The county fire department truck had arrived on the highway above followed by an ambulance and her undersheriff, Fred Lindholm. The fire crew quickly sprayed a thick layer of white foam over the burning vehicle. After a few tense minutes, the flames were beaten down.

Mandy sat rocking the baby while the EMS crew checked the driver. The men exchanged pointed looks and gave a brief shake of their heads.

Looking down at the child she held, Mandy's heart went out to him. Poor little baby. Was the woman his mother? Where was his father? Did he have anyone in the world to care for him?

Dressed in a blue-and-white sleeper, he looked to be a little boy maybe four or five months old. She combed her fingers through the silky fine blond curls on his head. "I wish I could have saved her, too."

Fred, a burly man in his late fifties, arrived at her side huffing with exertion. "I couldn't believe my eyes when I saw you crawling out of that burning car. Talk about a stupid stunt!"

Fred rarely missed a chance to criticize her, but she was too emotionally spent to defend her actions.

"You're bleeding," he pointed out, his tone softening slightly.

Glancing down, she saw blood on her sleeves. "I must have cut myself on the glass."

One of the EMS crew came to check the baby. Mandy bit her lower lip, reluctant to give him up. Holding the child kept her hands from shaking.

It was hard not to think about how easily they both could have died.

At the paramedic's gentle coaxing, she gave the child over, but noticed how empty her arms felt without his weight. She clasped her hands around her knees to disguise their trembling.

After rolling up Mandy's sleeves, a second paramedic cleaned her cuts, wound a roll of gauze around both her elbows and secured them with tape. She listened to his instructions on keeping the wounds clean and dry without comment. When he was done, Mandy rose to her feet, happy to find her legs were steady enough to stand.

She needed to get to work. There was an accident to investigate, reports to file, next of kin to be notified. Keeping busy was the best way to keep her mind off her close call.

Turning to her undersheriff, she said, "Get started with the scene, Fred. I want to know how fast she was going when she hit that railing. I'm going to take Emmett's statement."

She climbed the rocky slope to where the rancher was sitting in his pickup. When she reached him, she offered her hand. "Thanks for all your help, Emmett. I need to ask you a few questions for my accident report, but it shouldn't take long. Then you'll be free to go."

"It wasn't an accident, Sheriff."

That got her full attention. "What do you mean?"

He pointed to a hilltop off to the west of the road. "I was in the pasture, putting out protein blocks for my cows. I heard a crash,

16

and when I looked this way, I saw a dark pickup flying down the road beside that car. Plain as day, he hit her again, and that was when she went off the road."

"You're saying it was deliberate? Did you get a license plate number?"

"They were too far away. The truck stopped and a fella got out. He walked back and looked down at her, then he ran to his truck and took off."

Mandy pulled a gray notebook from her hip pocket and flipped it open. "You said a dark pickup. Was it black, blue? What model? Ford, Chevy?"

"My eyes aren't as good as they used to be. It wasn't light enough for me to see the color clear. I think it was a black Ford, but I can't be sure."

"Can you describe the man you saw?"

"He was a white guy. Tallish. He had on a dark cowboy hat."

Tallish with a cowboy hat. Emmett had just described two-thirds of the men in her county. Cowboys were as common as fleas at a dog park here in the Kansas Flint Hills where ranching was the main occupation. And ninety-nine percent of the men drove pickups.

"Which way did he go?"

"Toward town."

Fred drew her attention with a shout. He held up a black purse. Mandy excused herself and walked over to her officer.

Fred handed her the pocketbook. "This must have been thrown out of the car. The vehicle has Sedgwick County plates. I'm having Donna run them now."

Inside the cheap vinyl handbag, Mandy found a few cosmetics, a tan wallet and a date book. Opening the wallet, she located a driver's license. The photo matched the dead driver. Her name was Judy Bowen, age twenty-five.

Only two years younger than I am.

The license listed a Wichita address. Mandy hoped it was a current one. It would make it easier to notify next of kin.

Also in the wallet were two pictures of the baby. Mandy turned one over. *Colin, four weeks old,* was written on the back. She glanced toward the ambulance. So his name was Colin. It was a good strong name.

Other than thirty-three dollars and some change, there was nothing else of interest in the wallet. Mandy pulled out the date book, opening it to today's date.

A notation said, *Meet Garrett at the ranch.*

Mandy had lived in Timber Wells for the past eight months, but Fred had lived here all his life and he'd worked for the previous sheriff. She held out the book. "It appears the driver was Judy Bowen. Does the name Garrett ring a bell?"

Fred's eyebrows shot up. "Sure. Garrett Bowen lives about ten miles on the other side of town. She's his ex-wife. She left him about a year ago."

An interesting bit of information. "Did you know her?"

"I picked her up for possession of meth right after she moved out of his place. She pleaded out for community service, never did any time. She left town after that. I never heard anything more about her."

"What about the ex-husband?"

"I seem to recall they were both busted on drug charges down in Oklahoma a few years ago. I'd have to look it up. He hasn't stepped out of line in this county — that I know of — but I never did trust him."

"Why?"

"He's got a funny way of looking at you. Like he's looking through you. It ain't right."

"Emmett says the car was deliberately run off the road."

Fred handed back the book. "According to those skid marks she was heading away from his ranch not toward it. Maybe her visit with her ex didn't go so well."

19

"I'm thinking the same thing. What else do you know about him?"

"Not much. He lives by himself. I see his truck and trailer going through town at least once a week."

"He doesn't happen to drive a dark-colored Ford, does he?"

Fred nodded. "Come to think of it, he does."

Mandy watched as the coroner's hearse pulled up behind the squad cars. "Fred, notify the Highway Patrol. I'd like them to process the car."

"You think I can't do it? I've been working accidents since before you were born."

Rather than take offense, she chose to mollify him. "That's why I want you to stay and see that it gets done right. You know as well as I do we'll get the crime scene reports back faster if we let the KHP assist us on this."

"And what are you gonna be doing?"

"I'm going to get cleaned up, then I'm going to pay Mr. Bowen a visit. He wouldn't be the first ex-husband to settle a marital score with murder."

Mandy knew that all to well.

Garrett pulled a bent nail from the pouch at his waist and laid it on top of the wooden fence post. With careful taps of his hammer, he straightened it. Using his elbow to brace the next board against the post, he hit the nail, hoping it wouldn't bend. It went in straight and sure.

"See that, Wiley? All it takes is finesse." He glanced at the shaggy black-and-white mutt sitting near his feet. Wiley cocked his head to one side and wagged his crooked tail.

Garrett straightened another rusty nail, but it bent like a wet noodle when he tried to hammer it in. He tossed it into a nearby bucket of similar failures. The dog dashed over to nose the contents.

"Laugh at me, Wiley, and you'll go to bed without supper."

The dog leaped to his hind legs and pawed the air as he turned in an excited circle and yipped. The words *breakfast, lunch* or *supper* all brought about the same reaction. Wiley had a thing about food.

"Just kidding, buddy." Having suffered that punishment more times than he could count as a boy, Garrett would never inflict it on Wiley. He and the little stray had a lot in common. They both knew what it was to be beaten, hungry and abandoned.

"I may not have enough money for new lumber, but I reckon I can afford kibble."

21

Garrett stared at his half-finished corral. For now, he had to make do with used boards and nails salvaged from an old shed, but with a little luck and hard work, next year would be different. His herd of Angus cows might be small, but they were producing some fine calves this spring and prices were good.

Careful saving and the extra money he'd started earning as a cattle buyer would let him add to his herd in the coming months, but there wouldn't be cash left over to fix up the place.

He didn't mind waiting.

Pushing his hat back, he paused to lean both arms on the post and survey the green rolling grassland sweeping toward the horizon. Someday, these hills would hold hundreds of fat black cows with calves at their sides, all wearing his brand.

It was the one dream he held on to.

The month before Garrett turned eighteen, his alcoholic father died of a stroke. Garrett had inherited a nearly worthless house, two hundred and fifty acres of pasture and a mountain of debt. He'd had nowhere to go and no reason to stay — except that he loved the land.

Nothing about the prairie was closed up or shut in.

He loved the wide sweep of the horizon and the way the wind sent ripples dancing through the long grass. He loved the smell of newly mown hay and the sight of cattle knee-deep in the emerald green pastures. He loved the freedom the wide sky offered. The land asked for nothing, promised nothing. It just was.

After ten years of scrimping and saving he'd been able to buy back most of the land his father had sold off. He owned almost a thousand acres now. With the right stock, Garrett knew he could build up a breeding program to be proud of. He had a good start, but there was still a lot to be done.

It was a dream Garrett hoarded carefully. Too many of his dreams had been squashed by people he'd trusted. Like his father and his mother. Like Judy.

It's better not to wish for too much. Better not to trust at all.

Garrett pushed away from the post. Self-pity wouldn't finish his fence. He glanced at the sun nearly straight overhead. Judy should have been here by now.

He still wasn't sure how he felt about her impending visit. Why was she so adamant about seeing him? Why now?

Still pondering the question, Garrett walked to his truck. Pulling a board from the bed, he eyed it to make sure it was straight. Wiley barked twice, then raced off down the gravel lane.

In the distance, Garrett recognized the sheriff's white SUV approaching. A feeling of unease settled like a rock in his stomach. Pulling a red kerchief from his hip pocket, he wiped the sweat from his face, then settled his hat low on his head and waited until the vehicle rolled to a stop a few yards from him.

There was no mistaking the woman behind the wheel. Miss Mandy Scott — big-city cop turned small-town sheriff — slowly opened the truck door. Garrett fought to quell the churning in his gut as old memories rose to the surface.

His mother had called the police a few times, but their visits had only made matters worse. When the cops were gone, his father made her pay dearly for her audacity. Garrett had been too young and too frightened to help her.

His mother took her husband's abuse as long as she could. Then one day, she just left.

The slamming of the truck door yanked Garrett back to the present. He waited as Sheriff Scott approached.

She wasn't tall, maybe five foot five or six,

but the way she carried herself made her seem taller — as if she were looking down on him instead of up at a man who had a good six inches on her. Her honey-blond hair was pulled back into a no-nonsense ponytail. Her mouth was pressed into a tight line.

Everything about her from the mannish cut of her blue uniform to the shine on her black boots seemed to shout that she was a woman in charge.

She would be pretty if she smiled. Not that she was homely — just intense.

"Afternoon, Mr. Bowen." Her tone was all business. Pulling off her sunglasses, she let her gaze sweep over him. He forced himself to remain still, but his gaze slid to the house.

Shame clawed at his gut. Cold sweat trickled down his back.

Mandy wanted the man to take off his hat. He was a person of interest in his ex-wife's murder. She wanted to see his eyes. The bright noon sun and the wide brim of his battered Stetson made it impossible.

"Afternoon, Sheriff." He kept his hands at his sides.

"Nice day, isn't it?" Keeping one eye on him, she moved toward his truck.

"Yes, ma'am."

"I see you're getting a new corral in." She glanced at the rag-tag assortment of boards in his truck. She could see where he'd pulled down one of his outbuildings. Several more looked ready to fall down, yet his barn was in good repair.

"Yes, ma'am."

He wasn't much of a talker. Now that she had a face to put with his name, she remembered seeing him in town a few times. A tall, lean man with midnight-black hair and dark eyes, he was attractive in a quiet sort of way.

He wore standard ranching attire. A dark brown Stetson that had seen better days, faded jeans over scuffed cowboy boots and a blue, western-style shirt with the sleeves rolled up. The taut muscles in his tan forearms and the sweat stains on his clothes told her he wasn't afraid of hard work.

His record had been clean since his out-of-state arrest for marijuana three years ago, but that didn't prove he was innocent. It might only prove that he'd gotten smarter.

He stood silently before her. The thing that struck her most was how still he was. Almost at military attention, he waited as she crossed the graveled yard toward his vehicle. The crunch of her boots on the crushed rock was the only sound except for the panting of the little dog that scampered at her feet.

She wished the man would take off his hat.

Strolling to the front of his truck, she noticed a number of deep dents and scratches. "You've got some damage up here."

"Yes, ma'am."

She waited in vain for him to explain. He didn't say a word, didn't move a muscle. Finally, she nodded toward the hood. "Care to tell me how this happened?"

"It's an old truck. It gets used hard."

Wow, two whole sentences. He's really loosening up.

Stepping back, she cocked her head to one side. "This midnight blue looks almost black, doesn't it?"

He didn't say "Yes, ma'am" this time. He said, "Is there something I can do for you?"

His tone was clipped, lacking any emotion. His stillness bothered her. Was he hiding something?

Garrett wasn't used to company — especially not the company of a pretty woman who happened to be a cop. She'd come for a reason. He wished she'd get to the point.

She gazed at him without flinching. "Do you know a woman named Judy Bowen?"

His unease flared like a grass fire. "Yes."

"How well do you know her?" Her question sounded nonchalant, but it wasn't.

"What's this about, Sheriff?"

"I asked how well do you know her?"

Something was wrong, but he sensed he wouldn't get answers from Sheriff Scott until she was ready to give them.

He forced his tense muscles to relax. "She's my ex-wife, but I figure you already know that."

Only the slightest lift of her eyebrows acknowledged his assumption. "When did you see her last?"

He clamped his teeth together. He didn't like sharing details of his personal life. "Judy split about a year ago. I haven't seen her since."

"I heard she was here today. What time did she leave?"

How did the sheriff know Judy was coming to visit? "She hasn't shown up yet."

"Care to tell me why she was here?"

"I told you, I haven't seen her yet." He kept his face carefully blank. He'd learned as a child not to show fear or anger or anything that would trigger his father's rage. Still, it was hard to hold back his growing concern.

"Is that so?" She clearly didn't believe him. Her eyes locked with his, seeking something. Weakness?

Never let 'em see you're scared. He could hear his mother's cautiously whispered advice.

Garrett raised his chin a notch. "I'm not answering your questions until you tell me why you're asking. What's wrong?"

Mandy's eyes widened. "Why would something be wrong?"

"Because you're out here, grilling me."

She folded her arms and leaned back slightly. "Your ex-wife is dead. What do you know about that?"

Two

Mandy scrutinized Garrett Bowen's face, paying close attention to every detail.

"Judy's dead?" The disbelief in his voice was the first crack in his armor that she'd seen.

His gaze dropped to his boots. The dog came over. Whining, the mutt rose and braced his front paws against Garrett's knee. After a long moment, Garrett asked, "How?"

A flash of sympathy darted through her, but she suppressed it. Her job was finding Judy Bowen's killer. Mandy pulled her notebook from her pocket and flipped it open. "Her car was deliberately run off the road. Where were you at seven o'clock this morning?"

He looked up sharply. "Here."

"Who can verify that?"

"Wiley."

Her eyes narrowed. "And who is that?"

He nodded toward his feet. "The dog. I don't get a lot of company."

Not much of an alibi, yet his words had a vague ring of truth. If he wanted to cover up his involvement in a murder he could certainly do better than make a dog his only witness.

"Care to tell me what Judy wanted to see you about?"

"I don't know," he stated quietly.

Once more her suspicions were aroused. "Your ex-wife was coming to see you after a year and you had no idea why?"

"That's right. I got a call from Judy a week ago. She said she had to see me — to tell me something she couldn't put in a letter or talk about over the phone."

"Didn't that seem strange?"

"It did, but I didn't pry." He stared at his boots again. "Were drugs involved in her death?"

"That's an odd question. Why do you ask?" She hoped pretending ignorance of his record would put him off guard. If she could, she wanted to catch him in a lie. It would help her decide if she believed anything else he'd told her.

"Judy — had a drug problem."

"Really. When was this?"

He waited for a long moment, then said,

"While we were married, and before I met her."

"I see. What about you?"

Glancing up suddenly, he said, "I was arrested once for possession as I'm sure you already know. You think I had something to do with her death."

She arched one eyebrow. "I never said that."

"You don't have to say it."

"*Did* you kill her?"

"No."

Again, she heard a ring of truth in his voice, but she wasn't willing to accept his word. She'd been wrong before.

Let me get this one right, Lord. Help me find justice for that little boy.

Deciding to press Garrett, she stepped closer. "I can see how things might have gotten out of hand. You had a fight. She took off. You followed. Maybe all you wanted to do was stop her. You never meant to send her car off the road."

"No." His stood absolutely still. He didn't so much as flinch at her accusations. The wall he kept his emotions hidden behind was thick and well-crafted.

Mandy swept a hand toward his pickup. "I'd like to collect a paint sample from your vehicle."

"Don't you need a warrant for that?"

"I can get one." It wasn't an empty threat. She knew Judge Bailey would grant her request, but she also knew he was gone on a fishing trip until the end of the week. She didn't intend to wait that long.

Garrett slipped his hands in his hip pockets. "Take anything you want if it will help find who killed Judy."

His cooperation added weight to her feeling that he might be telling the truth, but didn't completely sway her. He wasn't what she would call eager and willing to help.

Keeping one eye on him, she set about collecting the paint scraping, sealing it in an evidence envelope and tucking it in her shirt pocket.

When she was finished, she turned and walked back to her vehicle. With one hand on the door, she glanced over her shoulder. "Don't leave the area, Mr. Bowen. I'm going to have more questions for you."

Kathryn Scott opened the oven door and extracted a meat loaf with a pair of blue flowered oven mitts. "A murdered woman, an ex-husband with no alibi and a baby. This case sounds a lot like the one you worked in Kansas City just before your father died."

Mandy didn't need to be reminded of that fact. It had been rolling around in her mind all day. "It is similar to the Wallace case."

"Whatever happened to him?" Kathryn placed the pan on an iron trivet on the table.

Mandy, standing at the counter in her mother's cheery white-and-yellow old-fashioned kitchen, continued filling two glasses with iced tea. "He's serving life in prison for smothering his baby daughter. I — We were never able to prove he killed his wife."

"Life can be so terribly sad. Sometimes, it seems as if evil is winning."

"Sometimes it does," Mandy agreed softly.

She'd only been a homicide detective in Kansas City for a few short months when she caught the Wallace case. In spite of the fact that her partner thought the husband was guilty of his ex-wife's murder, Mandy believed the man's story and released him after questioning him only briefly.

If she'd been less trusting, less gullible. If she'd dug a little deeper, tried harder to break him, maybe his daughter would still be alive.

"Do you think Garrett did it?" Kathryn asked.

Mandy considered the question as she

carried the glasses to the table. She'd sensed Garrett's unease, but he seemed genuinely shaken when he heard his ex-wife was dead.

Her conscience pricked her for the way she'd delivered the news, but gauging his reaction was part of her job.

She still didn't know what to believe. His shock was the only bit of emotion she'd seen in the man. Something wasn't right about that.

But he hadn't asked about the baby. That as much as anything made her think he hadn't seen his ex-wife that day.

"I'm not ruling him out."

Mandy sat down and waited as her mother dished up slices of meat loaf. The mouth-watering smells of cooked onions, spices and barbecue sauce filled the kitchen.

Mandy had sent paint samples from Garrett's truck along with scraping of the paint transfer from Judy's car to the crime lab in Topeka. It would be a few days before she had the results.

"What's he like?" her mother asked suddenly.

Mandy thought about it before answering. He was a tense and disturbing man, but there was something about him, something she couldn't put her finger on.

He seemed so alone. As if holding still

could hold him separate from what was going on around him. He seemed incredibly lonely.

She shook off the fanciful notion. She wasn't about to share that image with her mother. Instead, Mandy said, "He's not what you'd call the friendly sort."

Her mother paused in the act of passing a bowl of green beans. Alarm widened her eyes. "And you went there alone?"

Mandy sought to reassure her mother. "Don't worry. I know how to handle myself."

"That's what your father used to say."

Mandy watched as a sad faraway look filled her mother's eyes. Kathryn Scott had been devastated by her husband's death. A decorated police officer with nearly thirty years on the force, he'd been shot and killed during a drug raid two years ago.

For months afterward, Mandy had worried that her mother's frail health would fail and she would lose another parent. When the job of undersheriff in Timber Wells became available, it seemed like a gift from heaven.

The move back to her mother's hometown had been a good idea. With the help of old friends and caring members from the community's tight-knit church, Kathryn had slowly regained her health and her interest in life.

Less than a month after accepting the job, Mandy found herself promoted from under-sheriff to sheriff when her predecessor died of a sudden heart attack.

Kathryn leaned forward to squeeze her daughter's arm. "I pray the Lord will look after you, and I know your father's giving Him a hand with that."

After saying grace, Kathryn began a monologue of her day. Mandy listened with only half an ear. Garrett's face kept intruding into her thoughts.

There was something perplexing about the man. For one thing, what right-minded cowboy kept a roving dust mop as a ranch dog? The little black-and-white ball of fur might make a coyote fall over laughing, but it sure wouldn't be able to chase one away from the livestock.

Kathryn began to butter a roll. "Have you had any luck solving the farm supply store robbery?"

Mandy forced her mind away from the puzzle that was Garrett Bowen. "Not yet."

Mandy might not miss the hectic pace of the Kansas City Police Department, but she did miss the crime lab people. It normally took days, even weeks to get reports on prints and evidence she had to send to the Kansas Bureau of Investigation labs for processing. The turnaround time on evidence was one of her biggest frustrations.

"Why would anyone steal so much camping fuel?" Kathryn asked.

Mandy knew and it sickened her. "To make meth. Illegal methamphetamine labs are a major drug problem. It's easy to make, easy to transport and so addictive that a person has to use it only once or twice to become hooked. Yet, the stuff they make it with is poison. I don't know why people don't get that."

Just thinking about the havoc the drug caused was enough to stifle Mandy's appetite. Last month, she had arrested a couple so high on speed that they were lying on a railroad track screaming in paranoid terror while their two young children watched. The kids hadn't been fed in days. They'd been living on scraps while their parents spent every dime they could beg, borrow or steal on the drug that was destroying them.

Unless Mandy could stop the flow of meth into her county, she was afraid she was seeing only the tip of the iceberg. Rural crime was on the rise, and her department had seen a sharp increase in drug-related arrests in the town. Far too many of those crimes involved teenagers.

Kathryn took a sip of her tea, then said, "I thought the number of meth labs dropped off once the state passed stricter controls on over-the-counter cold medications."

"They did — for a while. Instead of stealing the pseudo-ephedrine or ephedrine from the local drugstores, they're getting it off the Internet from Canada or Mexico."

Reports from narcotic units in both Kansas City and Wichita pointed to the fact that large shipments of meth were coming out of Mandy's area. She knew she had a major drug ring operating almost under her nose. She just couldn't pin them down. Yet.

Mandy ate in silence as she tried to figure out what she had missed. After a few minutes, she felt her mother's gaze on her and looked up. "What?"

"I said Candice Willow's daughter is expecting again."

"What will that be, her fourth?" Mandy forked a piece of meat loaf into her mouth and braced herself for another round of why-don't-you-settle-down-and-raise-a-family hints from her mother.

"Candice's daughter is the same age as you are."

"Really? She's been busy." Mandy tried to hold back her sarcasm but failed.

"Grandchildren are such a blessing." A heavy sigh followed Kathryn's comment.

Mandy studied her mother's carefully blank face without comment.

Kathryn took another sip of tea, then said, "Did I mention Candice's oldest son is coming for a visit. He's a doctor. A radiologist."

So that's where this was going. Mandy laid down her fork and laced her fingers together on the table. "I'm guessing he's single."

Kathryn brightened. "As a matter of fact, he is."

"Don't you dare try and fix us up."

"I never suggested such a thing."

Mandy rolled her eyes. "Grandchildren are a blessing. He's a doctor. Come on, Mom, I can read you like a rap sheet."

"Grandchildren *are* a blessing, and I'd like to have some of my own before I die. It wouldn't hurt you to go out on a date once in a while."

"Fine. I'll go out with the next guy who asks me. In case you haven't noticed, they're not exactly lined up around the block."

Mandy rose from the table and carried her dish to the sink. "If and when the right guy comes along, it will happen. If not, then that's okay, too."

"Candice's son could be the right one. How will you know if you don't meet him?"

As soon as he hears I'm a sheriff, he'll run the other way. They all do.

"Just meet him. That's all I'm asking," her mother continued with a slight pout, then changed the subject.

After clearing the table and loading the dishwasher, Mandy bid her mother goodbye and left. Walking down the porch to the next doorway, she unlocked her side of the duplex and went in.

The quaint two-story Victorian house with its wraparound porch had been remodeled into a duplex. It had turned out to be the perfect place for them. Living next door to her mother gave Mandy peace of mind and her mother a sense of independence.

Mandy stopped in the kitchen to check her phone messages. The machine showed a red 0. She'd left clear instruction that she was to be called if any new leads or new information on Judy Bowen's case became available. Apparently, none had.

Feeling unusually restless, Mandy turned around, snatched her car keys off the hook and walked out of the house.

The drive across town was short. Timber Wells boasted only four thousand residents

41

and a total of four traffic lights.

Pulling into a large parking lot, Mandy stopped and stared at the front entrance of the town's hospital. She could have called to check on the baby, but what she really needed was to see him — to make sure he was doing all right.

Inside the building, the nurse on duty gave her a room number. Mandy found the pediatric ward and quietly opened the door to room 222. An elderly woman sat in a wooden rocker, holding Colin. The baby was whimpering softly.

"How is he?" Mandy crossed the room for a better look.

"Fussy, but I would be, too, if I had a broken collarbone."

Mandy took note of the small sling that held one arm pinned to his sleeper. "I'm Sheriff Scott. I just wanted to check on him before I called it a night."

"I know who you are. I understand this little man owes you his life."

"I was in the right place at the right time, that's all."

"It was by the grace of God you were there, and it was a brave thing to do, young lady. Would you like to hold him awhile? I really need to get back to my other duties, but he cries whenever I lay him down."

Taken aback, Mandy shook her head. "Oh, I don't know. I'm not much good with kids."

"Nonsense. Anyone can rock a baby. Sit here." The woman rose to her feet, leaving Mandy little choice but to do as she was told.

Taking the baby carefully, she held his small, warm body close. He whimpered again. Mandy looked up in concern. "I'm afraid I'll hurt him."

"Be careful not to jar his arm, and he'll be fine. The nurse gave him something for pain in his last bottle. It should take effect soon. Once he's asleep, you can put him to bed." With a smile of encouragement, she left the room.

Slowly, Mandy relaxed and as she did, the baby's whimpering stopped. Before long, he drifted off to sleep. Instead of laying him down, she continued to rock him gently.

He was a beautiful child. His long eyelashes lay in blond crescents against his chubby cheeks. His tiny bow mouth made sucking motions as if he were dreaming about his next bottle.

Mandy smiled. The warmth of the emotions he evoked in her heart nearly took her breath away. She stared at his delicate face. It felt so right and natural to hold him in her arms. She began to hum a soft lullaby.

Perhaps one day she would have a child of her own. She'd thought there would be time to settle down after the academy and after getting her career started, but then her father had been killed and her mother had needed so much of her time.

Time was exactly what had slipped away. Now, Mandy was stuck in a small town where even the bravest of men hesitated to ask the sheriff out on a date.

"I shouldn't whine when my life is so full of blessings," she whispered to the little boy who slept in her arms.

She shouldn't, but sometimes it was hard always being the one in charge. Always looking to right the wrongs in other people's lives. It was harder still when she *couldn't* right that wrong.

She'd never be able to give this little boy his mother back, but she would do her best to see that justice was done.

An hour later — long after her young charge and her arm had fallen asleep — Mandy managed to tear herself away. Laying him down, she stood for a moment rubbing away the pins and needles until feeling returned to her hand.

Kissing the tip of her fingers, she gently touched them to his forehead. "Sleep tight.

I'll see you tomorrow night."

Smiling, she realized she'd just made a date with the cutest guy in Timber Wells. Too bad he was only four months old. Somehow, she was sure this wasn't what her mother had in mind.

Someone had tried to kill that beautiful baby. Someone had succeeded in killing his mother.

Mandy vowed she wouldn't let him or her get away with it.

Garrett turned his truck into a parking space in front of the county courthouse just after ten o'clock in the morning. It had been two days since he'd learned of Judy's death.

He sat for a long time staring at the modern one-story brick structure and the immaculate green lawn that surrounded it. Flags fluttered in the breeze from a pair of flagpoles to the right of the low broad steps. Wiley, his paws parked on the armrest of the passenger's side door, barked excitedly.

Garrett rubbed his palms on the top of the steering wheel. He didn't like confrontations, but the news of Judy's death followed by what he'd learned this morning left him reeling. Sheriff Scott had a lot of explaining to do.

Judy had a son.

A child who would grow up without a mother because she had been coming to see Garrett — and he still didn't know why. A heavy sense of responsibility settled in his chest. Try as he might, he couldn't dislodge it.

He knew what it was like to be motherless.

Why hadn't the sheriff told him about the baby? Could the child be his? According to Judy's pastor, the baby's age made it possible, but surely Judy would have told him she was pregnant with his child.

Like Garrett, Judy had lived a hard life. When they first met at a truck stop in Overland Park, she'd been nursing a cup of coffee and a black eye from her latest in a long line of boyfriends who used their fists on her face.

She'd looked so alone, so lost. Garrett knew exactly how that felt. When she turned her heartrending smile in his direction and poured out her sad story, Garrett found himself determined to save her.

And she let him. They'd married within a month.

His dreams of a family to love and cherish the way he'd never been loved soon evaporated. Judy had a serious drug problem. She stayed with him a couple of years, but not out of love.

Garrett had simply been her free ride until she found something better. One day, she was gone.

Like everyone he cared about.

Getting out of his truck and closing the door, Garrett faced the courthouse again. He didn't relish the idea of setting foot inside a police station. There were cells inside where men were locked away. Just the thought made his skin crawl. If he had a lick of sense, he'd go home and finish his corral.

Except he couldn't. He needed answers, and Sheriff Scott had them. Facing his fears, he walked up the steps.

Inside the building, he found the door marked with the sheriff's seal. He stepped into the room and saw a plump woman in her midfifties behind the counter.

Two deputies were seated at desks behind her. Garrett recognized Fred Lindholm, and his hands balled into fists.

The last time Garrett's mother had called for help, Lindholm had been the one to respond. His help amounted to telling Garrett's father to sober up and take it easy on his old lady. Less than a week later, Garrett's mother left for good.

Maybe if Lindholm had done his job and

arrested Garrett's father, things might have turned out differently. The coil of anger and fear inside Garrett wound tighter, but he knew better than to let it loose.

At the desk next to Lindholm sat a younger man with short red hair and wide serious eyes behind wire-rimmed glasses. His name tag said Ken Holt. Garrett didn't know him, but if he was anything like Lindholm, he'd be a good man to avoid.

"May I help you?" the woman asked.

Garrett shifted his attention back to the receptionist. "I'd like to talk to Sheriff Scott."

"She isn't in right now. Can I take a message?" The woman smiled, but it didn't reach her eyes. She lifted a large pink leather purse to her desktop and began searching for something.

"When do you expect her back?" Garrett asked.

She pulled a stick of gum from her purse, unwrapped it and popped it in her mouth. "That's hard to say."

Behind him, he heard the door open and a cool voice he recognized said, "Mr. Bowen, what are you doing here?"

He turned around to see Mandy framed in the doorway. Once again he was surprised by how pretty she was. The very air around her seemed charged with rare energy. The nameless fear that squeezed Garrett's throat eased.

He breathed in the scent of her freshly starched shirt. Beneath the smell of ironed cotton, he caught a subtle sweetness. Honeysuckle?

A tenacious vine with delicate flowers and a heady perfume that belied its tough nature. The description certainly fit the good sheriff.

Why did he find her so attractive? The answer eluded him.

He pushed the thought aside and got back to the reason he was here. "Why didn't you tell me about Judy's baby?"

Mandy walked past him and entered a nearby office. He followed her, determined to get a response.

A cluttered, heavy wooden desk occupied the center of the room. On the walls hung certificates and wanted posters and a large framed picture of a man in a police uniform with Mandy's slender build and square chin.

Crossing her arms over her chest, she stood in front of her desk and regarded Garrett with a steady stare. He had the feeling she was stalling for time, searching for a way to respond.

"Where did you hear that she had a

child?" Her tone was cold enough to frost the windows.

"Today when I called the minister she worked for to see about funeral arrangements, he asked about her son. Why didn't you mention she had a kid?"

Mandy shrugged. "I didn't think it was any of your business. *You* never mentioned she had a child."

"I didn't know." He kept the bitterness out of his voice with difficulty. Judy had always said she didn't want kids. Maybe she just hadn't wanted his kids.

The pain of that thought made him flinch. "Is he my son?"

Mandy's face softened for an instant, but the look was gone so quickly he wondered if he had imagined it. She shrugged. "I don't know. What do you think?"

He stuffed his hands in the front pockets of his jeans. "Judy wasn't home much the last month she lived with me. I think she was seeing someone else, but the baby could be mine. Can I see him?"

"No. This is still an open investigation."

"Do you have any suspects? Besides me, that is."

"I'm not at liberty to discuss the case."

His bottled-up anger slipped its leash. "I didn't have anything to do with Judy's death. Are you even looking for the person who did?"

"I resent the implication that I'm not doing my job." Her eyes snapped with suppressed irritation.

He couldn't back down. Not now. "Resent away. I want answers."

Mandy raised her chin. "Mr. Bowen, the best thing you can do is go home and let us do our job."

Once again, the pretty sheriff was throwing up a roadblock. If she hadn't been so eager to pin Judy's death on him, he might have accepted her suggestion.

No, if he was going to get answers, he'd have to get them himself.

"I'll find out what I need to know with or without your help, Sheriff."

Mandy took a step closer. "Don't get in my way, Mr. Bowen. If you do, you'll regret it."

THREE

"That one's gonna be trouble," Donna said as Mandy came out of her office to watch Garrett cross the street to his truck.

Mandy wasn't happy he'd found out about the baby. It wasn't like the child could identify his mother's killer, but that didn't mean he was safe.

She picked up the phone and dialed the number for the pediatric floor. Her encounter with Garrett brought her protective instinct rushing to the forefront. She needed to make sure Colin didn't get any unauthorized visitors.

After leaving instructions with the nursing staff to notify her office if Garrett tried to see the boy, she hung up.

For the past two days. she'd spent several hours each evening with the baby, reading Mother Goose stories he couldn't yet understand, singing songs that seemed to soothe him. This morning, she'd stopped in to visit before coming to work. Somehow, she knew she needed to see his bright eyes and dimpled smile before she started her day.

Colin had become firmly wedged in her heart. She wasn't sure how she felt about the idea that he might be Garrett's child.

Donna crossed her arms over her ample chest. "I don't trust Mr. Bowen any farther than I can throw him."

Fred and Ken came to stand beside Mandy. She looked at them. "Besides his arrest, what do we actually know about him?"

"Not much," Fred admitted. "His old man drank like a fish. He hit hard times after his wife ran out on him about fifteen years ago. He had to sell off some of the ranch. He died about ten years ago. I hear Garrett's been buying some of the land back, bit by bit."

"He doesn't go to church," Donna interjected.

Mandy folded her arms. "I've seen his ranch. It isn't exactly prosperous-looking. Where's he getting the money to buy land?"

Fred leaned his elbows on the counter. "We can look into his financial records."

Ken cleared his throat. "Besides ranching he's a cattle buyer on the side. My uncle has used him a few times."

Mandy glanced at Ken. "What does that entail?"

"If a farmer or a rancher is too busy or doesn't like traveling to the sale barns, he hires a fellow to do it for him. He'll give the buyer an order for so many feeder steers or so many heifers. Guys who do it full-time can make good money if they don't mind the travel."

Donna interrupted again. "All that traveling sounds like a good cover for running drugs."

Mandy held back a smile. At times, Donna could be overly dramatic. The dispatcher had moved from a small town in Missouri to Timber Wells the same time Mandy had. Her experience as a dispatcher in that state made her exactly what Mandy had been looking for, and she had worked out well in spite of her outspoken ways.

Planting her hands on her hips, Donna continued. "A man doesn't shun his own community unless he's got something to hide. I've got a bad feeling about that one."

Unsure exactly what her own feelings for Garrett were, Mandy turned around and picked up a file from the front desk. "I'll be out of the office for the rest of the day, Donna. You can get me on my cell phone."

Donna perked up. "Where are you going?

You know how I like to keep track of my people."

Mandy strongly suspected Donna's attention to details was part of her naturally nosy nature, but she did a good job even if she was prone to gossip. She'd proven to be an asset in the community, as well. She volunteered at the high school and at the Prairie View Community Church in her free time with at-risk youth.

"I'm giving a Meth Watch talk at the high school with Agent Riley of the KBI. After that I'm headed to Wichita to interview people who knew Judy."

Mandy was dreading the talk. Public speaking wasn't her gift, but keeping kids off drugs was a cause she believed in.

"Talking to most of those teenagers is a waste of time," Fred said with a scowl.

Donna nodded sagely. "I know you think your meth education programs can make a difference, but I'm not so sure. I sit with those kids in after-school detention three nights a week. Some of them will use drugs no matter what."

Mandy lifted her trooper's hat from the wooden coat tree outside her office door. "But some won't, and those are the ones I'm trying to reach. Besides, we need to get a lid on these robberies. We need tips on suspicious activity. We can't do it alone. If we don't get the community involved, things are just going to get worse."

Only Ken nodded in agreement. Donna and Fred merely exchanged skeptical glances.

Mandy knew there were kids she couldn't save. People turned to drugs for any number of reasons and no amount of education could stop it all, but if she saved one person, it would be worth all her time and effort.

As it turned out, the school talk wasn't as difficult as she feared. Many of the students seemed genuinely interested in helping law enforcement keep their community drug-free. There were a couple of jokers in the crowd who snickered and shouted out wisecracks, but for the most part Mandy felt she'd gotten her message across.

With Agent Riley to help field questions and present what the KBI was doing to combat the problem, the hour passed quickly.

The high school principal, Cedric Dobbs, stood waiting for them when they left the stage. "Thank you for speaking today. I'll see that your hecklers spend a couple of hours in detention. Especially Luke Holt. You'd think having an older brother who is a deputy would deter some of his rowdy behavior."

Cedric's voice held a ragged edge that made Mandy look more closely at him. In his early sixties, Cedric had been teaching in Timber Wells his entire life.

Today, his usually impeccable suit was rumbled. His thick white hair was mussed, as if he'd been running his hands through it. He looked like a man under a lot of stress.

Mandy smiled at him. "It wasn't as bad as I expected."

"These kids. I don't know what's going to become of this town. For two cents I'd quit this job. I'm nothing but a glorified baby-sitter. Excuse me." He left to stop escalating horseplay between two boys.

Agent Jed Riley, dressed in a dark suit and tie, offered Mandy his hand. "Nice speech, Sheriff."

She shook it. "Thanks. Yours was better."

"I've had more practice. What's wrong with Mr. Dobbs? He looks like he's ready to tear out his hair. I don't remember him being so down on his students."

"His wife has cancer." Mandy didn't know the woman well, but had met her a few times at her mother's Bible study class before she became ill.

Sympathy filled Jed's eyes. "No wonder he

looks like he's aged since I was here last year."

"According to my mother, his wife's doctor wants her on a new experimental therapy, but their insurance won't cover it. They've used up nearly all their savings. They even had to sell their house and move into a smaller apartment. Are you on your way back to Topeka now?"

"No, I've got another talk to give in Council Grove. Any new information on your homicide?"

"I'm waiting on crime lab reports from the Highway Patrol."

"The Kansas Highway Patrol has quite a backlog. You may be waiting a while. Did the hits we gave you on those prints at the farm supply store robbery take you anywhere?"

"What hits? I haven't gotten anything from the KBI on that case."

"Really? I'm sure my office faxed you the report."

"I haven't seen it."

"We came up with prints for a couple of small-time crooks named J. J. Fields and Daniel 'Spike' Carver."

"I know them. They're a couple of local hoodlums. I never got the report."

Jed drew his cell phone from his pocket

and dialed. Holding it to his ear, he said, "Connie, this is Jed. I need you to do me a favor. E-mail a couple of reports for me to the sheriff in Morrison County."

He gave her the details, then snapped his phone shut and smiled at Mandy. "You should have them in ten minutes."

"Thanks, Jed. I'll have one of my deputies bring in J. J. and Spike for questioning. It might be the break I've been looking for."

After leaving the school, Mandy pulled into the Turner gas station and truck stop near the south edge of town to fill up before making the two-hour drive into Wichita. The sky, overcast since early morning, discharged a brief sprinkle that left the air smelling sweet and clean.

The station, operated by Aaron Turner and Mike Peters, was a hodgepodge business that had been doing well since the pair bought it six months ago. A tall rusting fence of corrugated tin enclosed a salvage yard at the back of the property. The sign out front offered auto repair and tow services, as well as free coffee and a doughnut with a fill-up.

A half-dozen clunkers sat waiting to be fixed or junked beside the large garage at the back of the property. Several eighteen-wheelers idled in front of the diesel pumps.

The majority of the place's business came from catering to the over-the-road truckers taking a break from the long and sometimes boring Kansas highway. They didn't seem to mind that the coffee was stout enough to dissolve horseshoes or that the doughnuts were stale because the station owners managed to keep their diesel fuel price at least a nickel lower than the gas station in the nearest town.

As Mandy slipped the gas nozzle off the pump, she saw a semitrailer loaded with smashed cars pull up to the salvage yard entrance. Mike came out of the building to open the gate, but stopped short at the sight of her.

She lifted her chin in acknowledgment to the small, skinny man in greasy gray overalls. He dropped his gaze and quickly went about his business.

"Don't mind Mike, he's just shy." Aaron Turner appeared at the hood of Mandy's truck. Slightly above medium height with dirty, dark blond hair that needed trimming, he exuded the confidence his partner seemed to lack. His red shirt was unbuttoned halfway down his chest and tucked into tight-fitting faded jeans.

"Maybe he doesn't like cops," Mandy suggested.

"I think he has a crush on you."

Flabbergasted, Mandy didn't know how to respond. Aaron moved to take the pump nozzle. His hand brushed down her arm.

She drew back. "I thought this was the self-serve pump."

He leaned toward her with a knowing smile. "We try to give law enforcement special consideration."

Mandy doubted Fred, Ken or anyone else in her department had been treated to the man's too-familiar charm. She folded her arms over her chest. "My officers don't expect or condone special considerations."

Aaron's smile faded. "I meant no disrespect, Sheriff. Have you caught the man responsible for running that poor woman off the road?"

Hating to admit she had almost nothing to go on, she said, "Not yet, but we will."

"I heard her ex-husband is a suspect."

Shooting him a sidelong glance, Mandy asked, "Where did you hear that?"

"Oh, you know. People talk."

"We're still working the case."

"How about the farm supply store robbery? Any leads there?"

She didn't need reminding that her unsolved caseload was mounting. "We're checking into several leads."

"A lot of the merchants in the area are getting worried. Crime is going up."

"Do you have a point, Mr. Tucker?"

"Personally, I've got nothing against women police officers, but I thought you should know that some people are saying you can't do the job."

The smirk in his tone told her exactly how much he enjoyed repeating the gossip.

The pump dinged to signal her tank was full. Aaron replaced the handle. "Will that be cash or charge, Sheriff?"

"Cash, Mr. Tucker. And should anyone else be wondering if I can do this job, the answer is yes."

Fuming, Mandy climbed in her truck and headed down the highway. First, Garrett accused her of not doing her job and now, if Aaron Tucker was to be believed, the whole town was wondering if she was up to the task.

God, I know I can do this job, but I need your help. Give me something to go on.

Drawing a cleansing breath, she blew it out and felt the tension in her body ease. God was on her side. She should never doubt that.

She also knew what good police work was. The logical place to start solving Judy Bowen's murder was with the victim's coworkers and neighbors. The first name on her list of people to interview was the Reverend Carl Spencer, a pastor of a small church in a poor section of the inner city where Judy Bowen had worked.

Intermittent showers gave way to clearing skies on the long drive into the city. The country music flowing out of her radio did little to distract her thoughts. The person she couldn't stop thinking about was Garrett Bowen.

She was starting to believe he wasn't involved in his ex-wife's death. A guilty man would be laying low, trying to avoid drawing attention to himself, not walking into her office and demanding she do more.

His dark eyes, so wary and watchful, were impossible to read. At times, she felt he looked at her more deeply than other men did. As if he wanted to see some part of her she didn't show the rest of the world. As if he knew her tough attitude was a cover for feelings she didn't care to share.

At other times, he looked past her, as if afraid of what he saw.

Shaking off her preoccupying thoughts, Mandy was relieved when the outskirts of the city finally rolled into view. Finding her way to the South Broadview Community Church proved to be easy enough, but as she pulled into a pothole-filled parking lot, she couldn't believe her eyes.

Garrett stood, shaking hands with a small, white-haired man dressed in a dark gray suit. Garrett's dog, his pink tongue hanging out, sat between them.

Mandy threw open her truck door and slammed it shut before marching up to Garrett. "Bowen, I thought I told you to stay out of my way."

He stiffened. She sensed his defiance, but his reply was calm. "I'm here to visit with a friend of Judy about funeral arrangements. I'm not looking to get in your way."

If he'd just get good and mad, she'd feel better about him. His icy control made her wonder what he was thinking.

He wasn't breaking the law, but the urge to slap him in cuffs was getting stronger by the minute. His dog chose that moment to yip at her and beg for attention, straining at his leash.

Garrett pulled him back. "Behave, Wiley, or the sheriff will lock you up for disturbing the peace."

The black-and-white fur ball sat obediently, but his little body wiggled with suppressed excitement.

Mandy turned her attention to the elderly man who was watching them intently. She held out her hand. "Good afternoon, sir, I'm Sheriff Amanda Scott of Morrison County. Are you Pastor Spencer?"

He took her hand in a firm grip. "That would be me. I'm pleased to meet you, Sheriff, but I certainly wish it were under happier circumstances. Judy was a member of my congregation and a dear friend."

"I'm sorry for your loss, Reverend."

"Thank you."

"I'd like to ask you a few questions."

"Certainly."

She shot a sideways sour look at Garrett. "Is there somewhere we can talk in private, sir?"

Garrett tipped his hat in her direction. "Wiley and I were just leaving. Thanks for your time, Pastor Spencer."

"Certainly. I appreciate how difficult a time this is for you. Just know that Judy is at peace with our Lord at this very moment."

Mandy caught a glimpse of deep sadness in Garrett's eyes and saw a muscle twitch in his cheek. He didn't reply. He merely nodded and turned away.

"It's hardest on the ones who don't believe," the reverend said softly. "Now, Officer, what questions do you have for me?"

"I understand Judy worked for you."

"Yes. She started coming to church here about six months ago. It was her enthusiasm for our work with abused women and children more than her typing skills that prompted me to offer her a job."

Mandy fell in step beside the reverend as he began walking toward the church. "Did you know Judy had several arrests for drug use when she lived in Timber Wells and in Kansas City?"

"She was a very troubled young woman when I first met her. She'd witnessed the murder of a friend at the hands of their drug dealer. It was her friend's death and Judy's narrow escape that finally forced her to confront and kick her habit."

At the side of the church was a small stone bench. He sat and indicated the space beside him. "Were you aware that Judy had an inoperable brain tumor?"

Startled, Mandy shook her head as she sat down.

Pastor Spencer sighed heavily. "When she found out about her condition, she became determined to see that Colin was taken care of."

"What about the baby's father?"

"You're asking the same question Mr. Bowen asked. Unfortunately, I have to give you the same answer. I have no idea who

Colin's father is."

"Judy never mentioned him?"

"I did ask her once when she confided in me about her illness. All she said was that she had caused him enough grief and couldn't burden him with a child. I thought perhaps he was a married man with a family of his own, but that was only my assumption. Judy planned to place Colin up for adoption."

Mandy knew she should be saddened by the news, but she wasn't.

The reverend continued, "It was very important to Judy that Colin be raised in a family that shared the same faith she'd found such comfort in."

"Did Judy have any other family?"

"No, she was alone."

And now so was Colin.

The seed of an idea began to take root in Mandy's mind. *She* could care for him, raise him in a faith-filled home.

Was it possible? Maybe Garrett wasn't the father.

Adopting a child had never occurred to her before, but then, she hadn't met Colin yet.

There would be time to consider what such a move would mean later. Right now, she needed to focus on the case at hand.

"Did Judy have any enemies?"

"Not that I was aware of, but the man who murdered her friend was never caught."

Now that was some serious motive. "Do you know his name?"

"No, and neither did Judy. The Kansas City police were never able to locate him."

That meant the case was still open. Mandy made a mental note to get the case file and review it for leads.

"Judy was terrified this man would come after her. She hitchhiked out of Kansas City and ended up here. When I met her, she was living on the streets and struggling to stay off drugs. Our women's shelter was a Godsend for her."

"Did you ever hear her say she was afraid of her ex-husband?"

"No."

"What about money? Is there anyone who'd benefit from Judy's death? Life insurance — anything like that?"

"Judy was as poor as a church mouse. Believe me, I know how poor that is."

Mandy smiled. "You said that she planned to put the baby up for adoption."

"Yes, she had an attorney. Donald Victor is the man's name. I'm sorry, I gave Mr. Bowen the card that Judy kept in her desk drawer, but I'm sure he'll be listed in the phone book."

Bowen again. Mandy pressed her lips together to hold back a comment. She pulled her own card from her shirt pocket. "Thank you, Reverend Spencer. You've been a big help. If you think of anything else, please give me a call.

After leaving the church, Mandy used the computer in her vehicle to look up Donald Victor, attorney-at-law. The address was across town. When she arrived at the location, she wasn't surprised to see Garrett was there ahead of her. His dusty pickup, looking decidedly out of place, sat parked between a new silver Lexus and a cherry-red Corvette.

Wiley, tail wagging and tongue lolling, raced between the partially rolled-down windows, barking at anyone who came close. As a watchdog, he wasn't much of a deterrent, but then Mandy doubted a thief would pick the beat-up truck over the red beauty beside it.

At least Garrett had chosen a parking spot in the shade of a tall sycamore tree. The consideration for his pet raised her opinion of him a notch. One.

Pushing open the heavy glass doors with the firm's name painted in gold lettering, Mandy entered a spacious foyer. In the center of the room, lush green plants were artfully arranged in pots beneath a domed skylight. The faint trickle of water from a small fountain could be heard over low classical music playing softly from hidden speakers.

The thick navy carpet muffled her footsteps as she approached the receptionist seated behind a low counter.

"Good afternoon. How may I assist you?" The woman's voice was cool and cultured. Her perfectly manicured nails matched her red dress. Not a single hair dared spring free from the French twist at the nape of her neck. Mandy couldn't help wishing she were dressed in something other than her drab uniform. She quickly dismissed the vain thought.

"I'm here to see Mr. Victor."

The woman glanced at the computer screen. "Do you have an appointment?"

Mandy smiled. "No, but this is official business. Has Mr. Bowen already gone in?"

The woman relaxed and nodded. "Just a few moments ago. He was very insistent about speaking to Mr. Victor."

"Which way?"

"Down the hall. First door on your left." She picked up the phone. "Shall I let them know you're here?"

"Don't bother. Mr. Bowen will be expecting me."

Garrett glanced over his shoulder when the door behind him opened. The sheriff hadn't wasted any time getting here. She had a smile on her lips, but it wasn't a warm one.

He turned his attention back to Mr. Victor. The man was frowning at the woman who had just barged into his office.

Mandy came forward and extended her hand to the attorney. "Sheriff Amanda Scott of Morrison County, Mr. Victor. I'm investigating the death of Judy Bowen."

She parked herself in the black leather chair next to Garrett. "What have I missed?"

Garrett had to admire her brashness. "Not much. Mr. Victor was just telling me that he couldn't give me any information. Maybe he'll feel more comfortable talking to the law."

"I'm sure he will. You can go now, Mr. Bowen."

"I believe I'll stay. This concerns me as much as it does you." Garrett could do simple math. Judy left him a year ago. The baby was about four months old. He needed this man to confirm or deny what he suspected.

She said, "As Judy Bowen is deceased,

your attorney-client privilege no longer applies. Is that right?"

Mr. Victor looked somewhat relieved. "Yes, that's true, Sheriff."

"What can you tell me about her?"

"Not much, actually. She came to me two weeks ago, wanting information about placing her son for adoption."

"I've always understood that private adoptions are very expensive."

Mr. Victor sat back and laced his fingers together over his pinstriped suit. "There was no cost to Miss Bowen. All fees and expenses would be paid by the adopting parents."

The man had the look of a college quarterback gone to seed. A thick gold ring glittered on his right hand. The overpowering scent of his spicy cologne permeated the air. Everything about him and about his office told Garrett he enjoyed the money he made.

"And who are the adoptive parents?" Mandy asked.

"Judy had not yet selected a family. Kansas law requires that both parents of the child relinquish their parental rights. It was my understanding that she intended to inform the father in person of her decision and obtain his permission."

72

"Did she give you his name?" Garrett asked quickly.

The attorney opened the file on his desk. "Yes, I assumed you knew. You are listed as the child's father."

Garrett sank back in his chair, his mind spinning. It was true. He had a son.

Why hadn't Judy told him?

What did he do now?

His past hadn't exactly prepared him for parenthood. He had no idea how to raise a kid.

Should he let this lawyer go ahead with the adoption? Judy must have believed it was the best choice, but was it?

Old dreams, dreams he'd thought long dead, crept out of the box where they'd been hiding. To have a family of his own. What would it be like?

Mandy leaned forward. "Mr. Bowen could have blocked the adoption if he wanted, couldn't he?"

Nodding, the attorney replied, "Certainly."

Mandy shot Garrett a sharp look. "Mr. Victor, did Judy ever tell you that she had spoken to Mr. Bowen?"

"She never got the chance to talk to me," Garrett stated sharply. He didn't like the sheriff's new tone.

73

Her doubt was plain. "So you claim."

"You think I'd rather see them both dead?"

"I've known it to happen," she retorted.

Why wouldn't she believe him? "I never saw Judy. I didn't know about my son until this morning."

The attorney cleared his throat, pulling Garrett's attention away from Mandy's intense eyes. "Mrs. Bowen named you as the child's father on his birth certificate which makes you his legal guardian unless your paternity is contested. I hope you will consider fulfilling Judy's wishes."

He pushed a sheet of paper across the desk toward Garrett. "I can assure you that our clients are well-screened. He will have a wonderful life with two loving parents."

Garrett took the paper the man was offering. "What's this?"

"Parental rights relinquishment form."

Garrett stared down at the legal document. Now he knew why Judy had been coming to see him. She wanted his consent to let strangers raise their child.

Children needed tenderness and caring, things he'd never known. His childhood had been a series of beatings and worse. He wasn't fit to be a father.

Mr. Victor pushed the paper closer. "It

was Judy's dying wish."

Garrett looked from the man's florid face to the paper in front of him. Judy's dying wish.

To honor it, all Garrett had to do was sign his name.

FOUR

Mandy stared at Garrett's stiff back as he shoved open the agency doors and exited the building. She called after him. "Signing those adoption papers is the best thing you could do for him."

She knew he'd heard her. He simply didn't bother to reply.

It took her a second to catch up with his long strides. His stoic silence irritated her.

"It's what your ex-wife wanted."

Still no reply. He just kept walking.

"You're not really considering raising that baby by yourself, are you?"

He rounded on her, his face a mask of pain and anger, his eyes narrowed to icy slits. It was the first real and honest emotion she'd seen from him. She stopped, but she didn't retreat.

It was as if some hidden floodgate had finally opened and the words poured out of him. "Two days ago, I found out my wife was murdered. We were divorced and we hadn't spoken for almost a year, but I still cared about her. Today, I call to make funeral arrangements and I find out I have a son."

He pointed toward the building. "You and that slick-haired bottom-feeder want me to write him off like a bad debt without so much as seeing him. I can understand why that attorney is so anxious to get my autograph. He'll make money if I sign, but why are you so dead set on it?"

If you give him up, he could be mine.

Facing the real reasons she wanted Garrett to relinquish custody was painful and sobering. Instead of voicing it, she said, "I've seen enough kids suffer because they were unwanted burdens. Colin deserves parents who truly want him."

The mask suddenly dropped over Garrett's features again. He retreated into himself, but not before she caught a glimpse of some terrible pain in his eyes. The raw emotion shocked her.

Reaching toward him, she asked, "Are you okay?"

He flinched away from her hand, but didn't answer. He was hurting; she knew it, but didn't know how to help. She didn't know if she should help. A strange sympathetic impulse tugged at her heart.

She said, "You should take some time and think about what's best for the child."

Folding his arms over his chest as if holding on for dear life, he looked over her, not at her.

Now she knew what Fred meant about him.

His anger was easier to face than this blank silence. She chose a different track. "The pen you snapped in half was probably expensive."

Her abrupt change of topic seemed to throw him off balance. He blinked hard, but then his eyes locked with hers. "Who cares about a stupid pen?"

"Destruction of personal property is a crime."

He leaned toward her. "So arrest me."

Raising one eyebrow, she fixed him with a steely stare in return. "Don't think I won't."

He took a step closer. "Where's my son?"

Surprisingly, she didn't find his nearness threatening. Just the opposite.

She caught the clean smell of sun-dried denim from his shirt. Unlike Donald Victor, no expensive cologne covered Garrett's warm, musky, strictly masculine scent. Mandy licked suddenly dry lips.

He was close enough to touch. She wanted

to press her hand against his chest, to feel the beating of his heart under the fabric of his shirt. The urge to cup his cheek, to feel the rasp of his whiskers against her palm shook her with its intensity.

She wanted to ask about the pain he carried deep inside.

She gazed into his eyes. His pupils darkened and his expression softened. In that moment, Mandy knew he felt it, too. This strange and exciting bond between them wasn't one-sided.

He closed his eyes and the connection was broken. Mandy's sanity returned in full force.

Was she nuts? The man was a suspect in his ex-wife's murder.

Crossing her arms over her chest, she leaned back, forcing herself to ignore the unexplained attraction pulling her toward him. "The child is somewhere safe."

"Was he hurt in the wreck?"

"He had a few minor injuries."

He zeroed his gaze on her. "How minor?"

"A broken collarbone and some bruises."

His jaw dropped. "A broken collarbone? You call that minor? How soon can I see him?"

"I'll let you know."

He glared at her. "You can't keep me away

from my own son."

Unfolding her arms, she settled her right hand on her holster. Better men than Garrett Bowen had tried to intimidate her and failed. "I can and I will. The child is already in Social Services' custody, and you're a suspect in his mother's murder."

He pulled back a fraction and blew out an impatient huff. "If you had one shred of evidence, I'd already be in jail."

Unfortunately, he was right.

Spinning away from her, he crossed the last few yards to his truck and yanked open the door. Sliding behind the wheel, he stuck his key in the ignition, but didn't close the door or turn on the engine. Wiley eyed them quietly.

After several long seconds of gripping the wheel with both hands and fighting some internal struggle, he finally looked at Mandy. "What's it gonna take? What do I have to do to see my son?"

She exhaled slowly. Was he sincere about wanting to see his child or was it all a show for her benefit? Something told her it was real.

"Until I get a conclusive paternity test and at least the preliminary tests back on the paint from your truck, I'm not allowing a visit."

"How long will that take?"

"Hard to say."

His eyes narrowed into a sharp glare for an instant. She thought he was going to argue, but then he simply nodded. "Once I'm cleared, what happens?"

He sounded so sure he would be. Mandy's opinion shifted a hair toward believing him, but she'd been fooled before.

"*If you're cleared,* and it's certain that you're the baby's father, it will be up to Social Services to decide if you're a fit parent."

If she hadn't been watching him so closely she might have missed the way his knuckles turned white where they gripped the steering wheel. He turned his face away.

More than anything, she wanted to read what was in his eyes.

"Can I call and check on him?" His voice was level, almost toneless, as if he couldn't allow any more emotion to escape.

"You can call me. I'll pass along any changes in his medical condition."

Sitting up straight, he fixed his eyes over her head. They were expressionless, holding no clue to what he was thinking. "I didn't hurt him. I didn't kill Judy."

She arched one eyebrow. "Do you know how many times I've heard suspects protest their innocence? Care to guess how many times they were lying?"

His gaze slid to meet hers. "I'm not lying, but that doesn't make any difference to you, does it? In your eyes, I'm guilty until proven innocent. What if you never find out who killed her?"

"I don't give up easily, Mr. Bowen. I will find who is responsible."

"Make it soon. I'll call tomorrow to check on —" He stumbled to a halt. A fleeting look of confusion crossed his features.

"Colin," she supplied. "His name is Colin."

"Colin," he repeated softly. The barest hint of a smile pulled at the corner of his mouth. "I'll call and check on Colin tomorrow."

As Mandy watched Garrett drive away, she wondered why she wanted so much to believe he was innocent.

Garrett braked to a stop in front of his home and turned off his truck. Wiley whined to get out and pawed at the window, but Garrett didn't move. The same question had been tumbling through his brain since he left the attorney's office in Wichita.

Why didn't Judy tell me I had a son?

They had talked a little about having children when they were together. Judy wasn't keen on the idea. He knew she came from a rough home — the same as he did. He thought in time she'd grow to want children. Instead, drugs had taken over her life and pushed him out of it.

Wiley whined again and shoved his cold nose under Garrett's hand. Garrett pulled his thoughts back to the present and glanced down at the dog.

"I guess I'll never know what she was thinking. The real question is, what do I do now? Any suggestions?"

Wiley's reply was a wide yawn.

"You're a big help. Should I sign the adoption papers?"

Garrett thought he'd come to terms with spending his life alone. It was better than facing the pain of caring about someone and then having him or her walk out of his life the way Judy had — the way his mother had.

Only now, he didn't have to face life alone.

"I have a son." He said the words aloud, letting them sink in.

"The ranch will be his someday." The thought brought a quiet joy — an emotion so foreign he almost didn't recognize it.

Garrett turned back to stare at the square two-story ranch house and his pleasure faded. The tall narrow windows on the upper story stared back from beneath the gabled roof like vacant eyes. All the shades were drawn. All the secrets were shut up where no one could see.

Maybe it was time to face them.

He rubbed his suddenly cold hands on the thighs of his jeans. Wiley whined softly. Leaving the truck, Garrett climbed the steps of the porch. Wiley raced ahead and began his usual twirling dance in front of the door. Unlocking it, Garrett let the pup in.

Wiley made a beeline for his bowls on the rag rug at the side of the kitchen cabinets and began lapping at his water dish.

Garrett walked to three doors at the very back of the kitchen. The one straight ahead led to a small bathroom. The one on the left led to the basement. The door on the right was the one he never opened.

Reaching for the knob, his hand shook slightly. Seeing the fine tremor brought a sick feeling to his midsection. Would he ever lose this fear?

Grasping the brass knob firmly, he pulled open the door. Unoiled hinges groaned and creaked in protest. A rush of stale air carried the smell of musty rooms long closed off. He glanced up the dusty stairwell.

A storm of bitterness and fear twisted his stomach until the ache made him press a hand to his belly.

He hadn't climbed the steps in front of him in ten years.

Judy had made fun of him for leaving so much of the house shut off. He knew she'd explored the upper level when they were first married. She complained about not being able to open one closet. He told her the key had been lost. It was the only time he'd ever lied to her.

Since he'd converted an old parlor into a ground-floor bedroom long before they met, she rarely ventured upstairs after a month or so.

He knew what was up there — he just didn't like to think about it.

He started upward, his boots echoing on the wooden risers. At the top of the steps, the stairs ended in a short hall. Down the corridor, three closed doors, like silent sentinels, guarded the ghosts of his past.

He opened the first door on his right and looked into the room that had belonged to his parents.

It was empty. The hardwood floor was scratched and scarred under a layer of grime. Two oval voids on the walls showed where pictures had once hung. A large brown smear still stained the wallpaper beneath the window. His mother's blood. He closed his mind against the memory.

The click, click, click of doggy toenails on the bare wooden floor made Garrett look down as Wiley came in. The dog made a circuit of the barren room, sniffing as he went. He stopped at the window and rose on his hind legs to look out.

After checking the view, Wiley dropped back to all fours and came to sit beside Garrett. The dog's bushy tail swept an arch of the floor free of dust but raised a cloud of it into the air. Wiley sneezed twice. The knot in Garrett's midsection eased.

"There's not much to see up here." The sound of his own voice forced back the panic he felt.

Wiley's tail swung faster. He whined and licked his lips.

Gathering his courage, Garrett opened the room's closet door. A pair of shirts, a few worn dresses and a dusty black suit hung from wire hangers on the rod. Other than the clothes the space was empty. Garrett ignored the contents.

Reaching up, he felt along the shelf until his finger touched metal. He pulled an old-fashioned key down and left the room with it clutched in his hand.

Out in the hall, he walked to the next door on the right and stepped into the room that had been his when he was a child.

To anyone looking, it was just another empty room. Painted a pale blue with a cheap carpet remnant covering the center of the floor, it seemed like a benign space — unless someone knew where to look.

His pulse pounded in his ears as he crossed the room to the closet. His fist tightened over the key until it bit into his palm. Cold sweat beaded on his brow.

He couldn't make himself unlock the door. He took a step back.

It was better to keep it closed. Better to keep everything locked away.

Once more, the click-clack of toenails heralded the approach of Wiley. The dog paused on the threshold and whined.

Garrett turned away from the closet. Leaving the room quickly, he pulled the door shut then leaned his head against the panel until his racing heart slowed.

It was over. It would never happen again.

Turning his back on the room, he straightened and looked at the opposite door. He crossed the hall and opened it without hesitation.

This room had been a storage space for as long as he could remember. Crammed with broken furniture, rolled up rugs and numerous boxes, it smelled of old cardboard and dust.

Surveying the space, he nodded. If he decided to raise the boy, this could become Colin's room when he was older. No bad memories lingered here. It was just a room. This junk could be moved into the other bedrooms. It could be piled in front of the other closets hiding their secrets even deeper.

Was he really considering trying to raise his son alone? The pretty sheriff didn't think he had any business doing so. Maybe she was right. What business did he have pretending to be a father?

They'd never let him keep Judy's boy. He was crazy to think they might.

Don't hope for too much. Don't wish for too much. Someone will take it away.

Hope wasn't worth the pain that came with it.

Wiley parked his paws on Garrett's leg and barked.

"You're right. We should go. I'm sure you want your lunch."

The dog started yipping and hopping in excited circles.

A lonely cowboy and a nutty dog with a crooked tail. Both of them misfits in the world beyond this ranch. They had nothing but each other. Until today, it had seemed like enough.

Pointing toward the door, Garrett said, "Go on. I'll be down in a minute."

Wiley dashed into the hall and Garrett listened to him descending the stairs. Crossing the hallway back to his parents' bedroom, he replaced the key and left the room as he'd found it.

The ghost of his past couldn't be erased, but it was welcome to keep the top floor. At the bottom of the stairs, he pulled the door shut again and turned his back on the place where his nightmares lived.

Thursday morning, a week after her visit to Judy Bowen's attorney, Mandy sat at the cluttered oak desk in her office and stared at the crime lab reports in her hands. The only sound in the room was the crackle of paper as she flipped over a page and continued reading, then flipped back to read it again. Finally, she looked up at the man seated on the other side of the desk.

"The paint's not a match to Garrett Bowen's truck. It's cheap black spray paint, the kind you can buy at any automotive or hardware store. It's not going to help us much."

She wasn't sure if she was relieved or disappointed that she had no evidence to tie Garrett to the crime.

Thomas Wick, the county attorney, tapped his fingers on the arm of the chair. "I assume this lets Mr. Bowen off the hook."

A man in his midfifties, Thomas was neatly dressed in a dark blue suit over a pristine white shirt and a bolo tie with a large silver concho. He sat at ease in one of the brown leather wingback chairs that made Mandy's small office seem even smaller.

She closed the folder and leaned back, hoping her frustration didn't show. "For now. The paint on his vehicle is original from the factory. He had motive. He had opportunity. It would have been nice to tie this up in a neat package. Instead, I'm back to square one. Who wanted Judy Bowen dead and why?"

"Maybe it was a simple case of road rage."

She gave a slight shake of her head. "Maybe, but my gut tells me there's more to it. Have you been out to the site?"

"Of course."

"Then you might have noticed her car ended up in the deepest ravine anywhere along that highway. I think someone knew the road and knew exactly where to run her off."

"What about the murder she was supposed to have witnessed in Kansas City?"

"I had Donna request the files on the case, but we haven't received them yet."

"Social Services will be pushing to find placement for the baby. I understand he can be released from the hospital soon."

Mandy nodded. "I talked to their social worker this morning. The paternity test is conclusive. It's Garrett's child."

"Because we're not swearing out an arrest warrant for him, we can't keep him from his son much longer."

Drumming her fingers on the desk, Mandy said, "I've got no legal reason to keep him away, but the situation is a recipe for disaster. He should honor his ex-wife's wishes and go through with the adoption. A man like that doesn't have a clue about raising a baby."

"Single parents raise children all the time," Thomas chided.

Mandy shook her head. "It's not that."

"Then what is it?"

"The man is hiding something. I feel it in my bones. He has one arrest for drugs —"

"That was three years ago. Nothing since then. His financial records don't show anything out of line. We've got nothing tying him to his ex-wife's death."

Mandy knew that as well as Thomas did. "Something about the man has me puzzled, but I can't put my finger on it."

She'd already lost enough sleep over Garrett's behavior, over the way he could shut off his emotions at the drop of a hat. Was she projecting guilt onto him because the case was similar to one she'd blown years ago? No, it was something more.

She steepled her fingers on the desktop. "If he keeps the baby, I'll be keeping a close eye on both of them."

Tom blew out a long, slow breath. "I'm afraid that's all anyone can do at this point. The nurses at the hospital tell me you've been over every night to tuck in the little fellow."

Embarrassed that her emotional attachment had become common knowledge, Mandy tried to shrug off her involvement. "I feel responsible for him. Besides, he's adorable. He has the sweetest smile."

And a dimple in his cheek like his father.

True to his word, Garrett had called every day for an update on Colin's condition. Each time she talked to him, Mandy felt her resistance to him crumble a little more. If only she could be *sure* he was innocent.

Having been so wrong once before, she wasn't willing to take that chance again. Colin's life might depend on it.

"Any other cases I should know about?"

Tom asked.

Pushing her conflicting feelings about Garrett to the back of her mind, Mandy went over the cases that needed Tom's attention. "Besides a few traffic tickets and a dispute between neighbors over some cows on the highway, the county has been quiet for the past few days. The only major arrest we've had is that young couple on burglary charges that I brought in yesterday."

"Is it a solid case? Never mind, that was a stupid question. You always bring me solid cases. You do good police work, Sheriff. We're lucky to have you."

"Thanks." Praise from Tom was high praise, indeed.

Rising to his feet, Tom said, "I'll be in my office if you need me. Do you want to notify Social Services that Bowen's been cleared or shall I?"

"I'll do it."

At the door, he paused with his hand on the knob. "I've been meaning to ask how things are working out between you and Fred Lindholm? I know there was a lot of resentment on his part when he was passed over and you were appointed sheriff."

"Sometimes Fred's attitude isn't the best, but I think we're making it work."

"I'm glad to hear that."

After he left the office, Mandy added her findings to the file she already had on Judy Bowen. At the sound of a knock, she looked up to see Fred enter.

She asked, "Have you had a chance to interview J. J. Fields and Spike Carver about the farm supply robbery?"

"They claim they had legitimate reasons for being in the store."

"And you believed them?"

"They're both working as tow truck drivers for Turner's Truck Stop. They claim they were in the store to pick up new work gloves and that's how their prints got there."

Puzzled, Mandy asked, "Why would Aaron Turner hire a pair of shady characters like J. J. and Spike? Does he know they have arrest records?"

"I assume he does."

"Don't assume, Fred. Check."

His scowl deepened, but he didn't comment. He just turned on his heels and left. Donna poked her head in when he was gone.

"Sheriff, Ken called to say he's going to be a half hour late this morning."

Mandy had a hard time containing her annoyance. "Again? That's the third time in a month. Did he give you a reason?"

"He said he overslept."

"If he keeps this up, he and I are going to have a chat."

Donna took a step into the room. "Is that the report on the paint sample? What does it say?"

"The paint isn't a match to Bowen's truck."

"That doesn't mean he didn't do it. It just means he was driving a different vehicle."

"I thought of that, but I've got no proof that he had access to another truck."

Dragging a hand through her hair to get it out of her face, Mandy wondered what she was missing. Her whole focus was on Garrett. He'd become an obsession and she wasn't sure why.

"I may be looking in the wrong place on this. Did K.C. ever send the files on the murder investigation I asked for?"

"I haven't seen them."

"Request them again. I'm not going to rest until I find out who left that baby to die in a burning car."

FIVE

Garrett was on his way out the door when the phone rang. Knowing he had a busy day ahead of him, he considered letting the machine pick up, but decided against it. It could be about Judy or about Colin.

Oddly, he hoped the caller would be Mandy. He'd spoken to her every day for the past several days. He'd gotten to where he actually looked forward to the calls.

There was something deeply comforting in the sound of her voice.

This time, the female on the other end of the line wasn't Sheriff Scott. "Mr. Bowen, this is Shari Compton. I'm Colin's social worker."

"Yes, ma'am." Here it came, the news that Judy's baby wasn't his son or that he wasn't fit to raise him.

"The paternity tests results are in. The child is your biological son."

"He's mine?"

The tangle of emotions that shot through Garrett took his breath away. Relief, joy, terror.

"Yes," Miss Compton continued, "I'm calling to tell you that you've been granted supervised visitation."

"Does that mean I can see him?" He tried not to get his hopes up.

"Yes."

His surge of happiness was followed quickly by apprehension. Things were never this easy. "When?"

"Today at noon is the only time I have available. I'm sorry for the short notice."

He glanced at the clock. It was already a quarter of eleven. He needed to be in Junction City at the sale barn at one o'clock. He had an order for forty heads of feeder cattle that needed filling today.

His client was new, but had the potential to give Garrett a lot of business and some much-needed referrals.

A cattle buyer's livelihood was directly related to his reputation. A buyer who couldn't fulfill his contract was one who'd soon be out of work. The extra income Garrett earned was important to his plans for the ranch.

A ranch he could hand over to his son one day.

The idea took hold and wouldn't let go. He didn't have to spend his life alone. He had a son.

Provided he could gain custody of Colin.

Telling the social worker he was too busy to see the boy today wasn't the place to start. "I'll be there."

"Good. I'll see you then. We can talk after you've had a chance to visit with your son."

An hour later, Garrett walked into Timber Wells Medical Center with sweaty hands and a pounding heart. At the front desk, he was told to wait. He took a seat on one of the chairs lined up beneath the wide window overlooking a shady stretch of lawn and fidgeted with his hat all the while wondering if getting his hopes up was a bad idea.

What if this woman decided he wasn't suitable? What if he couldn't take care of a child? What if he was like his father?

Would she be able to tell that?

A tiny middle-aged woman in a dark gray tailored pantsuit walked up to him. He shot to his feet and wrestled down his panic.

She held out her hand. "Mr. Bowen, I'm Miss Compton."

He wiped his damp palm on his jeans before taking her hand. "Pleased to meet you."

"I will be supervising your visit today.

Tomorrow, I'll be making a home visit to assess your ability to care for and house Colin."

"Tomorrow?" He swallowed hard. How much of the house would she need to see?

Concern clouded her eyes. "Is that a problem?"

"No, ma'am. Is it all right that I have a dog?"

A small smile lightened her features. "I'm not a dog person myself. I would request that you keep him confined during the home visit, but unless he eats small children, I don't think he will be a problem. I'm not the enemy, Mr. Bowen."

"No, ma'am." He wanted to trust her, but trusting people was hard for him.

"I really do have Colin's best interest at heart. Social Services has programs that can help you with medical expenses, parenting classes, even food and housing."

"I'm not looking for charity."

"It isn't charity. These programs benefit many families. If you'll follow me, I'll show you the way to Colin's room."

As the woman bustled down the hall ahead of him, Garrett relaxed a little. Maybe this wasn't going to be as bad as he thought.

When they reached the baby's room, a nurse in pink scrubs was waiting for them just outside. "My name is Glenda and I'm Colin's nurse today."

She opened the door and walked in. After a moment of hesitation, Garrett followed.

The room was decorated in shades of blue and tan with a flowery border along the top of the walls. A television, suspended from the ceiling, was tuned to a channel that played soft music as messages about parenting and health classes flashed across the screen.

In the far corner of the room sat a white metal crib with a large wooden rocker beside it. All he could see in the crib was a lump of blue terrycloth.

"Do you have any questions for me?" the nurse asked.

Garrett almost laughed. A million, but he didn't know where to start.

He stepped up to the crib. The lump was a baby, sleeping on his stomach with his legs drawn up beneath him and his little rump sticking in the air. Garrett drew a sharp breath into his suddenly tight chest.

The boy's head was covered in soft, blond hair. His cheeks were plump and pink and he was sucking on his thumb.

Whatever Garrett had been expecting, it wasn't this feeling of warmth that spread through him like sun-drenched honey. "He's so . . . small."

The nurse and the social worker exchanged smiles.

"He won't stay little for long," a familiar voice added. Garrett looked over his shoulder to see Mandy standing in the doorway.

She was in uniform once again, a light blue shirt with a shield-shaped patch on one sleeve, dark blue trousers with a yellow stripe down the legs. Around her waist, she wore a thick black belt and the tools of her trade, a holster, a slim baton and a radio. He assumed she had handcuffs, but they must be in one of the small leather cases on the belt.

The only thing different about her today was her hair. It was loose about her shoulders, giving her a softer, more feminine appearance.

Not that she needed much help in that department. Once a man got past the fact that she carried a gun, she was really easy on the eyes.

The baby began to stir, and the nurse said, "He's waking up. Mr. Bowen, have you ever given a baby a bath?"

He'd managed to wrestle Wiley into a tub once a month, but he was pretty sure that wouldn't count. He shook his head. "No, ma'am."

"In that case, I'll show you how. Let me get my supplies."

Mandy stepped into the room as the nurse left. "Mind if I watch?"

He did. He didn't want another witness to his ineptness, but would Miss Compton count it against him if he objected?

He glanced at the social worker but couldn't read anything in her face.

"Don't mind a bit." He tried to smile, but couldn't quite manage it. He still held his hat in his hands. Glancing around, he spied a small table and walked over to set it down. He didn't like being the center of attention, but it seemed he didn't have a choice.

When he walked back to the crib, he found Colin regarding him with wide bright blue eyes.

Judy's eyes.

He's beautiful, Judy. Why didn't you tell me about him?

Sudden tears blurred his vision, but he quickly wiped the wetness away, hoping no one noticed. He glanced toward Mandy and Miss Compton, but their attention was on the door as the nurse came back in with a blue plastic tub and several towels.

"All right," Glenda said brightly. "Let's get the little fellow undressed."

Garrett awkwardly turned the baby on his

back, so he could undo the snaps of the sleeper, but Colin was no help. He kept arching his back and trying to roll onto his stomach. Finally, Garrett simply had to brace his forearm across the baby's chest and hold him down while he undid the fasteners.

None of the women in the room spoke or offered help. Was he being too rough?

Garrett looked at the nurse. "I thought he had a broken collarbone."

"He does, but babies heal much more quickly than adults. Be careful not to pull on his left arm. He'll let you know if you're hurting him."

When he had the snaps undone, Garrett slipped the garment off his son's arms and legs, seeing for the first time the boy's chubby, stout little body.

Glancing at the nurse, Garrett said, "He looks like he's going to be a football player."

Suddenly, a warm wetness hit the front of his shirt. He jumped back in surprise.

Chuckling, the nurse handed Garrett a towel. "I should have warned you — he's armed and dangerous."

Brushing at the wet patch, Garrett returned her smile. "I'll remember that."

With the nurse's help but knowing both Mandy and Miss Compton were watching,

Garrett managed to transfer his son into the tub. Keeping the squirming, slippery baby upright in the water was tough. Bathing Wiley, with all its pitfalls, was a piece of cake compared to this.

Colin's head bobbed back and forth making it even harder to hold on to him. He kicked joyously in the water and tried to flap his arms, making occasional squeals. Each time he did, Garrett flinched, sure he was hurting the boy. No doubt Mandy and Miss Compton were making mental notes to that effect and wouldn't give him custody.

The disappointments Garrett had known in his life should have kept his hopes at bay, but they didn't. Not now that he'd met this grinning, squealing, splashing little man. This was his son.

They belonged together.

When he finished sponging the soap off Colin, Garrett lifted him to a dry towel and wrapped him up. Colin, bereft of his watery playground, focused on Garrett's face once more.

Garrett had never believed in love at first sight, but gazing into his son's sparkling eyes, he knew this was as close as it got.

The nurse said, "Now you need to get him dressed."

Over the next five minutes, Garrett

struggled to get his damp, determined-to-remain-naked son into a diaper and a sleeper. Bulldogging a calf was easier. The sticky tabs on one side of the diaper ripped when he pulled it tight and he had to start over with a new one. Then, the snaps of the sleeper didn't line up. It took Garrett three tries before he got it right. By this time, Colin had begun to cry.

All the while, Garrett was conscious of eyes boring into his back, judging his every move.

How badly was he doing? How much leeway would he get because he'd never dressed a kid before?

When he finished, the nurse told him to sit in the rocker, and he gladly followed her orders. Then she handed him a bottle and plunked Colin in his lap and stood back. "Go ahead and feed him. I've got to see to my other patients."

Just like that?

Garrett watched her walk out of the room and then looked down into the solemn eyes of the infant studying his face.

Don't let 'em know you're scared.

It was good advice when dealing with bullies, horses and strange dogs. Maybe it worked with kids.

Miss Compton said, "Sheriff, will you be

here for a few minutes?"

Mandy nodded, and Miss Compton smiled her thanks. "I need to make a notation on Colin's chart. It won't take long." She left the door open as she exited the room.

Garrett saw Colin's lower lip began to quiver. He gave one little fuss, then let out a holler that startled Garrett into nearly dropping him.

"Careful." Mandy quickly stepped in to steady the baby. Squatting on her heels in front of Garrett, she helped him position the baby into the crook of his arm.

"Thanks." Garrett finally managed to get the nipple into Colin's mouth. The minute he did, Colin stopped crying and latched on, using his chubby hands to pull the bottle closer.

Mandy stroked the baby's hair. "That's all you wanted, isn't it, honey?"

Her eyes softened when the baby turned his attention to her.

"Do you have kids?" Garrett normally wasn't one for small talk, but he couldn't help wondering about the woman who tried to be a hard-nosed sheriff, yet went all soft at the sight of a baby's smile.

"No." Her single-word answer was filled with wistfulness.

Neither one of them said anything else. They simply watched Colin until he began drifting off to sleep as he neared the end of his bottle. When it was completely empty, Garrett set it aside. Kids needed burping or something, didn't they? The nurse hadn't come back yet.

Unsure of exactly what to do, he shifted the baby to his shoulder and was rewarded with a hearty burp that left a half-dollar-sized wet spot on his best shirt.

Mandy rose to her feet, struggling to keep a straight face.

Garrett rose, too, and carefully returned Colin to the crib. Mandy pulled the blanket over the sleeping infant.

Glancing sideways at her, Garrett found her watching him intently. He couldn't help speculating about what she was thinking.

He was thinking how pretty she would be if she let herself smile.

Heat rose in Mandy's cheeks at Garrett's close scrutiny. The air between them simmered with charged expectation. He was too close. The scent of leather and warm male skin teased her senses, making her want to lean closer, breathe deeper.

Instead, she forced herself to move away.

She couldn't find fault with Garrett's

behavior toward Colin. The grim determination on his face as he'd tackled his son's bath had been almost comical. The tenderness she saw as he laid his son back in bed would have been hard to fake, but would it last? Would he be able to manage when things got hard?

She'd given another single father the benefit of the doubt once. When he failed, his innocent child paid the ultimate price. It wasn't a mistake Mandy was willing to make again.

"Sheriff, this is Fred. Do you read me?" The voice bursting out from her radio startled her and woke Colin. She grasped the mic. "Go ahead, Fred." She located a pacifier and handed it to Garrett who began to soothe the baby.

"I just got a tip on an active meth lab."

Another one? Where was it going to end? "Do you think it's a good tip?"

"The best. An off-duty police officer. He says they're cooking in an old trailer. Number 41 on Glenville Road."

"That's on the far side of the lake."

Mandy glanced at Garrett. He stood watching her intently. She turned and left the room, but stopped outside in the hall. "Are you sure about the location?"

"Johnny grew up here before he moved to

Topeka," Fred explained. "He was in his boat, fishing off Glen Point, and claims he got a good whiff. He knows the smell of meth cooking."

"Okay. I'll contact Judge Bailey for a search warrant. I want at least two more deputies on this. Have dispatch call Ken Holt and Benny Mason and meet us at the station. I'll be there in five minutes. I want everyone in Kevlar vests. If this *is* the gang that's been moving so much meth, they may be armed."

"Understood."

Garrett walked into the hall. "Was that about Judy?"

She shook her head. "When I have something new to share, I'll find you."

Miss Compton came down the hall toward them. "Mr. Bowen, I need a few more minutes of your time."

Glancing at his watch, he frowned. "Can it wait until tomorrow?"

"I'm afraid not."

He didn't look happy, but Mandy didn't have time to worry about him. She was already heading out the door.

Twenty minutes later, she and her men were gathered in the sheriff's office. Carefully, she mapped out how she wanted the raid to go down. When she was sure everyone understood their jobs, she tossed Fred the keys to the truck. "Let's go get the bad guys."

Fred grinned. "Yes, boss."

As they walked outside to their vehicles, Mandy saw Garrett zoom past in his truck on the way out of town. He wasn't headed toward his ranch.

Fred said, "Wish I'd had my radar gun on that one. Wonder where he's going in such a hurry?"

Mandy wondered the same thing, but quickly dismissed Garrett from her mind. She had more important things to worry about. Like the safety of her men.

Once inside her truck, Mandy picked up the mic to make sure everyone was in radio contact. "Central, do you read me?"

"You're breaking up, Sheriff." Donna's voice came over the set.

"We read you loud and clear," Ken said from the other vehicle.

Mandy hesitated. The last thing she wanted was to be out of touch with the office. There was no telling if they would need additional backup. "Donna, what seems to be the trouble?"

After a long moment of silence, Donna said, "I can hear you now."

"All right. Let's go."

They made the ride in silence until they turned onto the gravel road that curved around the far side of the county lake. The trucks kicked up clouds of white dust as they sped along. Mandy rehearsed the approach they would take once they arrived. It was impossible to be prepared for everything, but she tried.

Fred pulled to a stop several hundred yards from the trailer where a thick stand of trees and underbrush shielded them from view. Mandy stepped out and the others joined her.

She said, "Remember, these people are handling potentially deadly chemicals. Our goal is to get everyone out of the trailer. If they are cooking meth, we'll cordon off this area and get the KBI down here with a hazardous materials team. Anyone who touches a suspect or their clothing needs to be wearing gloves. Is that clear?"

As everyone nodded, she pulled on her own pair of latex gloves and pointed to Fred. "You and Benny circle around the back of the property. Tell me when you're set and wait for my signal."

"Let me go around back," Ken suggested. He smiled weakly. "I'm not as allergic to poison ivy as Fred is."

Mandy glanced toward the dense underbrush and nodded. "Okay. I don't care who
takes the back."

While the men worked their way around
to the rear, she pulled a bullhorn from the
backseat of her vehicle, then she and Fred
approached the front of the trailer.

Keeping under cover by crouching behind
a row of cedars at the end of the lane,
Mandy surveyed the area. It looked de-
serted. There were no vehicles, no signs of
activity, but she caught the pungent scent of
ammonia and propane in the air. It sure
smelled like someone was cooking meth.

She waited impatiently for her deputies to
get into position.

After several long minutes of silence,
Mandy grew irritated. What was taking so
long? She spoke into her handset. "Ken, are
you ready?"

He didn't answer.

"Ken!" she hissed.

Finally, his crackly voice came back.
"Sorry, boss. I'm set. I have the back door
in sight."

"Can you see any movement?"

"Nope."

"Benny, are you in place?" she asked.

"Yes, Sheriff."

"All right. I'm going in."

Mandy moved across the weedy unkempt lawn and stopped behind an overturned wooden boat with a gaping hole in the hull. Fred crouched beside her, his gun drawn and trained on the doorway.

Raising the bullhorn to her lips, she said, "This is the Morrison County Sheriff's office. Come out of the trailer now with your hands in the air."

No one responded. Nothing moved.

She spoke into the horn once more. "This is your last chance. We have a warrant to search the premises. Come out with your hands up."

Mandy waited for another full minute. Still nothing.

It was time to act. Signaling Fred to cover her, she laid down the megaphone and drew her gun. Cautiously, she approached the trailer, alert for any movement or threat. Adrenaline coursed through her body. Her nerves were stretched wire-thin.

She was only a few feet from the front door when the trailer erupted into a fiery ball. The blast sent her flying backward.

Six

Mandy sat on the rear bumper of the ambulance with an ice pack pressed to her smarting face. The bitter taste of ash clung to her lips. Flexing her jaw, she tested the limits of her injury. According to the EMT, she was going to have a nasty bruise. From the sting in her cheek, she knew he was right.

A plume of dark smoke rose above the trees in front of her. The fire department had the flames under control in a matter of minutes, mostly because there was nothing left to burn by the time they arrived. The ancient trailer by itself had been a death trap of flammable materials. Added to that, the volatile ingredients of speed and it became a bomb.

All that remained now was a burned-out hulk in a scorched circle of earth amidst the dense saplings and underbrush.

Fred was stretching yellow crime scene tape across the area. Ken was still making a sweep of the property, looking for suspects. No one had gotten out of the trailer unless they'd done so before Mandy arrived.

When the fire chief walked up, she braced herself. "Was anyone inside?"

He shook his head, and she relaxed. "Thank God for that."

"You should be thanking God you didn't get to the door a minute later."

"Believe me, I am."

"It was a trap."

She scowled at him. "What do you mean?"

He held out the remains of a charred timer. A pair of electrical wires dangled from the melted plastic case. "The place was deliberately rigged to blow. My guess is that someone knew you were coming and detonated the place to destroy the evidence."

She blew out a long, frustrated breath. "Looks like they succeeded."

"Residue tests positive for meth. It was an illegal lab, no doubt about it. I'll get this case to the KBI crime lab. Maybe they can lift a print or DNA from it."

It was a slim chance, but it was all they had. "Thanks, Chief."

"At least you know you didn't miss them by much."

"How's that?"

A grim smile cut through the grime on his face. "It's only a fifteen-minute timer."

As he walked back to his crew, Fred and Ken returned to her side. She lowered the ice pack. Ken whistled. "Bet that hurts."

She gingerly replaced the cold compress. "Did you find anything?"

Ken shook his head. "No, and that's what's weird. The property is secluded and heavily overgrown with brush. It would be a perfect dumping ground, but I didn't find a single empty jug or propane bottle. If they were cooking speed here, they went to a lot of trouble to keep the place clean."

She looked at Fred. "What about you?"

He shook his head and fingered the bandage on his forearm. "Nothing. The gravel doesn't hold tire tracks or footprints. But the next time we do this, I'm gonna take my chances with the poison ivy and Ken can rush the door."

Ken drew himself up in indignation. "I was doing you a favor."

"Don't do me any more."

Mandy held up a hand. Her head ached enough without having to listen to the two of them argue. "Let's figure out how they knew we were coming."

"They could have had a lookout," Ken suggested. "A two-way radio and someone on the high ground. I'll check out the likely places."

"So there had to be at least two of them," she mused.

Fred lifted his arm to wipe his face with his sleeve. "They could have been tipped off."

"By whom?" It was hard to focus with the pounding inside her skull in addition to her aching face.

"Bowen was driving in an all-fired hurry in this direction just before we left town."

Ken shook his head. "How could he know we were coming here? Even if he was using a scanner, we weren't using the normal radio channel."

Mandy's heart dropped a beat before thudding into fast forward. Garrett *had* overheard her radio conversation with Fred. Was it possible he was involved?

She didn't want to think so. Having seen how gentle he was with Colin, she couldn't believe he could rig an explosive that might kill someone less than an hour later.

She jerked her head toward the road, then winced as the movement brought more pain. "Where does this lane go?"

Ken raised his arm to point. "It circles around the lake and comes out about a mile down the highway."

"So whoever was here had an escape route planned, knew how to rig an explosion and knows how to keep evidence to a minimum. We're not dealing with some small-time crooks. This is a professional job. These guys are smart."

"Which explains why Kansas City claims big shipments are coming out of here."

Big drugs meant big money. Mandy couldn't figure out why they didn't have a money trail. None of the merchants in town were reporting strangers making expensive purchases or locals with more cash than normal.

"What we need is more manpower," Ken stated firmly.

"Dream on," Fred scoffed.

He was right. Besides her two full-time deputies, she had only three part-time men to help cover a county of more than nine hundred square miles made up of rural farms, ranches and a few tiny towns. Their budget wouldn't stretch to provide more men. Even the fire department was made up of mostly volunteers.

Like a large portion of Kansas, her countryside was dotted with abandoned farmsteads, barns and dense wooded gullies, hundreds of places where illicit drug makers could set up shop without being seen.

Places like this trailer.

Where would they set up shop next? Hopefully, outside of her county. She rubbed her aching neck. What she wouldn't give to be one step ahead of them instead of two steps behind.

Ken laid a hand on her shoulder. "Are you sure you don't need to go to the hospital?"

She dropped the ice bag on the floor of the ambulance and stood. "I'm sure."

"Why don't you let Benny drive you back to the office. Fred and I can finish up here. You've had a rough week. It wouldn't hurt you to take the rest of the day off."

Burning cars, exploding trailers — Mandy did feel beat-up, but she wasn't one to shirk her job. "I'm fine."

Fred's brow settled into a scowl. "I can handle this."

Ken stepped closer. "If it was one of us, you'd make us go."

Knowing Ken spoke the truth, she nodded in resignation. "I think I will go back, but call me if you find anything."

"Yes, boss," Ken agreed with a grin.

Fred didn't smile, but he did begin barking orders to the firemen still raking through the ashes.

The ride back to town jolted every sore muscle in Mandy's body. If it was this bad now, she wasn't looking forward to tomorrow.

At the office, Donna's plump face knitted into a sharp frown as Mandy walked in. "Good grief! Are you okay?"

"I'd be better if you had two aspirin somewhere in one of your magic bags."

"Aspirin, ibuprofen, band aids, chewing gum, I've got about everything." She drew forth an enormous leopard-print purse. At least three times a month she came in with a new bag. Donna was a self-proclaimed shopping network addict.

"Just the aspirin."

Digging into the shoulder bag, Donna came up with a bottle and shook two white tablets into Mandy's outstretched hand. "I heard they got away."

"Yes, they did, but we didn't miss them by much. They'll slip up again and we'll nab them."

"Any leads?"

"Not yet. The fire chief recovered the remains of a timer. We're sending it off to have it checked for prints."

"Where are the men?"

"Benny brought me back. I sent him home. Ken and Fred are still out at the site."

"For how long?"

"For as long as it takes, Donna." Mandy

didn't mean to sound exasperated, but all she wanted to do was sit down somewhere dark and let the aspirin do its job.

It was clear she'd ruffled the dispatcher's feathers. "You know how I like to keep track of my people. Maybe I can't be out in the field with you, but I can do the best possible job right here."

"You do a great job, Donna. No one keeps better tabs on this county than you do."

Relaxing a bit, Donna inclined her head. "Thank you. Shari Compton called. I put her through to your voice mail, and your mother called."

"Did Mom say what she wanted?"

"No. She just said for you to give her a call when you got the chance."

Mandy wasn't looking forward to *that* conversation. There was no way around it. Her mother was going to hear from someone about the explosion. It would be better coming from Mandy than from some second- or thirdhand source. "Anything else?"

"Nope."

"The case files on the murder Judy Bowen witnessed should have been here by now. Have you seen it yet?"

"No, I haven't. You know how those big-city departments can be. They move at the speed of refrigerated molasses."

"They aren't usually this slow. Could you please e-mail them a reminder?"

"Sure thing, boss."

Nodding her thanks, Mandy walked into her office and closed the door. Settling into the padded black chair at her desk, she picked up the phone and listened to her message.

"Sheriff, this is Shari Compton. I'll be making a home visit to assess Garrett Bowen's place in the morning. I received a copy of his background check. Thank you. There won't be a need to have an officer accompany me tomorrow. Mr. Bowen's visit went very well today. I'll get a full report back to you in a day or two. Goodbye."

Mandy chewed the corner of her lip as she pressed the delete button. Because Garrett had one uneventful visit with Colin didn't mean he was the best option for the child's future. She had no illusions about the child welfare system. While she didn't doubt Miss Compton's intentions or her commitment to the children assigned to her, Mandy knew that like everyone in her office the woman was overworked. She would want Colin's case settled as quickly as possible.

Mandy's county didn't have its own social

worker. There simply wasn't enough money in the state's budget or people willing to take on the job. When Mandy's office did have a child in need of care, a worker was assigned from another county. Very few enjoyed the long drive to her town. Sometimes, they didn't even know how to find Timber Wells.

Colin Bowen wasn't going to fall through the cracks of the system and end up in a questionable home if Mandy had anything to say about it.

She punched in the numbers to return the woman's call. When Miss Compton picked up, Mandy got right to the point. "This is Sheriff Scott. I'll be going with you to the Bowen place tomorrow. What time is our meeting?"

When Garrett answered the knock at his front door the next morning, he'd been home exactly ten minutes. Expecting to see Miss Compton, he tried to hide his surprise at the sight of Mandy standing on his porch.

The sight of fresh bruises on her face brought back sharp memories of his mother.

The thought of someone hurting Mandy the way his mother had been hurt sent a spurt of anger through him. It was followed closely by bitter guilt. Someone had failed to protect Mandy the way he'd failed to protect his mother.

He hadn't given much thought to how dangerous the sheriff's job could be. Mandy always seemed in control, as if nothing fazed her. Seeing her now made him more aware than ever that she was a flesh-and-blood woman.

A woman he found himself attracted to in spite of how foolish that was. He pushed aside the thought and schooled his voice into neutrality. "What happened to you?"

"Irate egg timer."

He stepped back as she walked into the house. "Most people blame it on a door."

After her eyes swept the room, she turned to face him. "I'm not most people."

No kidding. *Most people* didn't set his pulse racing or make him aware of how empty his life was.

"I was expecting Miss Compton this morning."

"I'm sure she's on her way. Don't mind me, I'm just here as an observer."

Tipping her head slightly, Mandy subjected him to closer scrutiny than he liked. She said, "You don't look so good. Tough night?"

His fast trip to the sale barn in Junction City yesterday had resulted in only twenty heads of cattle instead of the promised forty because he'd arrived so late. He'd had to travel on to a second sale in Concordia adding two hundred miles to what should have been a forty-mile trip.

The only good thing was that he got the remaining cattle he needed at a price that would make his client happy. After that, any good luck he still had ran out.

On the way home, his truck died, leaving him stranded twenty miles from nowhere. He'd hitched a ride into the next town and got a tow, but the repair shop owner didn't have the parts needed to fix it. Garrett had to wait until the local auto parts store opened this morning.

Once he had the Ford running, he'd headed home at top speed. The last thing he'd wanted was to cancel this visit or show up late and maybe lose his chance to get his son.

He ignored Mandy's comment about his haggard appearance. "So how does this *home visit* go down?"

"Miss Compton will answer that for you."

"Do you come along on all her visits?"

"Frequently. Believe it or not, there are people who don't like social workers."

"And you think I'm one of them."

"Did I say that?"

He folded his arms over his chest. "Why are you really here?"

"I want to be satisfied that you can provide a good home for Colin."

"Isn't that Miss Compton's job?"

"*I* want to be satisfied."

He glanced around. "I'm not much of a housekeeper."

She wandered from the entryway into the kitchen. "I don't see any blatant health violations."

He tried to view his place through her eyes. The vinyl flooring was old, but it was clean. Wiley made sure every crumb that hit the floor was taken care of. The cabinets were simple pine, but scarred with years of use. The countertops were chipped and stained. Duct tape on one corner held a loose section of edging in place.

He said, "It's not fancy, but it's been good enough for me and the dog."

The question now — would the social worker think it was good enough for his son?

Once again, he tried not to get his hopes up.

Mandy walked toward the rear of the room. Garrett shoved his hands in his pockets and kept his gaze away from the door that led upstairs.

She glanced at him and a subtle change

came over her features. His heart hammered in his throat. Did she know he was hiding something?

Another knock signaled the arrival of Miss Compton. Garrett had to turn his back on Mandy to answer it. It was one of the hardest things he'd done in a long time.

Briefcase in hand, the little woman smiled as she greeted him. "Good morning, Mr. Bowen. How are you?"

"Fine." His mouth was dry as August dust.

She seemed to know it. "Please don't be nervous."

Easy for her to say. He managed a smile. "Why don't we step into the living room?"

"Thank you." She walked in and took a seat on his sofa.

Garrett looked over his shoulder just as Mandy started to open the bathroom door. "No, don't do that!"

His warning came too late. Wiley, freed from his temporary holding cell, paused only long enough to sniff Mandy's boot before making a beeline for the living room. Garrett tried to intercept him, but the dog evaded capture and launched himself into Miss Compton's lap.

She pushed ineffectively at the excited animal trying to lick her face. "Oh, no! Bad dog! Get down!"

Garrett rushed to her aid. "Wiley, heel!"

With one last doggy kiss for his new, if reluctant friend, Wiley scrambled off the couch and dropped to his haunches beside Garrett, looking utterly pleased with himself and waiting for praise.

"I'm sorry about that, Miss Compton. He's not used to company."

Mandy entered the room, looking sheepish. "I didn't realize he'd been shut in the room when I opened the door."

Bending down, Garrett scooped up his pet. "He'll settle down in a minute."

Miss Compton brushed at the dog hairs on her black dress. "As I told you at the hospital, I prefer you keep him shut up or outside while I'm here."

"Yes, ma'am." Garrett shot Mandy a reproachful look.

Spreading her hands wide, Mandy muttered, "Sorry," as Garrett walked by.

How was she to know he had his pooch locked up? And for good reason it seemed. She'd seen a look of growing concern on his face when she approached the rear door. It was in her nature to assume he had something to hide.

So what if this time she'd been wrong. It didn't happen often.

Miss Compton finished plucking lingering bits of fur from her suit, removed a pad of paper from her briefcase and began jotting notes.

When Garrett returned, minus the dog, he took a seat in the wingback chair beside the sofa. Leaning forward, he braced his elbows on his knees and clasped his hands together. "Wiley won't be a problem with Colin."

He looked like a man waiting for the ax to fall.

Mandy hadn't considered how hard this had to be for him, having strangers judging his fitness to be a father. She'd been concerned only with Colin's welfare. In spite of her effort to remain impartial, her compassion for Garrett began to grow.

Miss Compton cleared her throat. "I hope you're right. Let's begin by my asking you a few questions."

"Yes, ma'am."

Mandy listened to Miss Compton quiz Garrett on his readiness to assume care of his son and formed a few opinions of her own. Garrett never relaxed, never offered more than he was asked, but he answered everything with a readiness that proved he'd given a lot of thought to what having a child in his home would mean.

After Miss Compton finished with her inquiries, she went over the needs Colin would have and what programs were available to help low-income families. Garrett listened intently, asking few questions of his own.

While Miss Compton was talking about health care, Mandy used the time to study Garrett's home. The living room was sparsely furnished with a blue floral-print sofa and fake bamboo end tables. The chair he sat in was dark blue, oversized and masculine in style. It was the only piece in the room that seemed to fit his personality. Perhaps Judy had furnished the rest of the room.

Glancing around, Mandy was struck by the lack of family photos and knickknacks in the room. It was almost spartan. Not very homey, but not the worst place she'd seen kids being raised.

When Miss Compton finished her interview, she withdrew another folder from her case and opened it. "If it is all right with you, Mr. Bowen, I'd like to take a quick tour of your home."

"Okay. What would you like to see?" He didn't rise.

Miss Compton smiled encouragingly. "For starters, where will Colin sleep?"

"I figured I'd put a crib in here for him."

"In here?" She looked around.

"Yes, ma'am." He jerked his thumb over his shoulder. "My bedroom is through that door. I thought, until the boy was older, I should keep him close by so I could hear him at night."

"That's good thinking, Mr. Bowen. May I see your kitchen? You'll want to make sure all your cleaning supplies and chemicals are kept out of reach. I have a pamphlet here on childproofing the house."

He rose slowly to his feet and led the way to the kitchen. "I'm gonna get that counter-top fixed soon."

"That's fine." The social worker moved toward the bathroom door.

Garrett started forward. "I shut Wiley in there again."

She took a step back. "I see. I'll take your word for it that you have adequate bathroom facilities. Where do these doors lead?"

Garrett stepped forward and opened the one on the left. "This is the basement. Not much down there but my washer and an old workbench. I reckon I'll need to get a lock on this door before Colin gets big enough to go exploring."

"Yes." She turned around. "And this door?"

He didn't answer. His body tensed. His eyes darted to Mandy and back to Miss Compton. He pushed his hands deep in his pockets.

"That leads to the upstairs," he said in a rush. "I only use that part of the house for storage."

Mandy glanced at the ceiling. "You use the whole upper level for storage?"

"Just one room. The others are empty. I'll fix it up before Colin gets old enough to need his own room."

"Mind if I take a look?" Mandy asked.

A shuttered look slipped over his face. "The door sticks. I've been meaning to plane it down."

That wasn't permission. Mandy chafed at the fact that she couldn't search any farther without a warrant. Why didn't he just invite them to explore? Because he was hiding something. Mandy didn't think it was his bad housekeeping.

"Are we about done?" Garrett asked.

"Are you in a hurry to get rid of us?" Mandy countered.

"Judy's funeral is this afternoon. I need to leave soon if I'm going to make it."

Wincing inwardly, Mandy tried not to show it. Wiley began barking from his place of confinement. Garrett looked at Miss

132

Compton. "That means he needs to go out."

She grimaced. "I believe I have everything I need."

"Don't you want to see the upstairs?" Mandy turned the knob hoping to urge Miss Compton in that direction.

She was doomed to disappointment. Miss Compton glanced at her watch. "I see no reason to view unused storage rooms. Mr. Bowen has adequate space in the house. It's in good repair. I'm satisfied. I really must be going. I have a long drive ahead of me."

Turning to Garrett, the social worker held out her hand. "You'll hear from my office officially in a day or two, but I see no reason why Colin can't be released into your care when he's able to leave the hospital."

A genuine smile cracked his features for the first time. His whole body relaxed as he gripped her hand. "That's great."

Mandy wasn't sure she was ready to accept Garrett Bowen at face value. Outwardly everything seemed okay. Her gut told her there was more to the man than met the eye.

Unfortunately, it didn't tell her how she was going to discover the rest of the story.

The crackle of her radio was followed by Donna's voice. "Sheriff, are you free?"

"Yes, Donna, what's up?"

"We got a call about a fertilizer theft out on Range Road."

Not another one. "That's on the other side of the county from me right now. Where's Ken?"

"That's just it, Sheriff. I can't locate him."

SEVEN

Two hours after getting the call that Ken Holt was missing, Mandy faced her errant officer as he shifted nervously from foot to foot in front of her desk. The tension in the room was thick enough to cut with a knife. His personnel file lay open before her.

She laced her fingers together and prayed for wisdom. "You have a decision to make, Ken."

"I'm sorry. I had a personal thing come up that I needed to take care of right away. I should have called to let you know, but I thought it would only take a couple of minutes."

Mandy ignored his rambling excuse and started again. "You have a decision to make, Ken. Either you're going to be part of this department and conduct yourself accordingly, or you're going to be looking for work elsewhere."

"I know I messed up, but I'm a good officer."

"I used to think so until you started showing up late for work. Your paperwork has gotten sloppy, and now going off the clock without telling anyone where you are, that's not acceptable."

"I said I was sorry."

Closing the file, she rubbed her forehead. "Sorry isn't good enough, Ken. I need your assurance that when I call for backup, I'm going to get it."

"You have it," he insisted quickly.

Opening the bottom drawer of her desk, she searched for and found the form she needed and began to fill it out. "This reprimand constitutes your first written warning, Ken. It will remain part of your permanent record."

"Is that necessary?"

She looked up sharply. "Yes, it is."

His gaze shifted to the floor. "Of course."

"Your pay will be docked for the time you were unavailable, plus you'll pick up an additional shift this weekend. If your personal problem is something you need to talk about, I'm here to listen. If you need time off, tell me now, and we can work something out."

"It's nothing I can't handle."

She allowed concern to soften her voice. "All right. I'll take your word for it, but if you need help, all you have to do is ask."

"Yes, ma'am."

She finished filling in the details on her paper, then turned it around and slid it across the desk toward him. "You'll have to read this and then sign it. It states we've talked about the following issues."

He scrawled his name, dropped the pen on her desk and then straightened and stared directly ahead. "Will that be all?"

She nodded knowing she couldn't do anything to help until he was ready to talk about what was wrong. He turned abruptly and left the room.

Slipping the signed form inside his file, she couldn't help wishing Ken felt he could confide in her.

"You were kinda rough on him," Fred said, walking in uninvited.

"He's a big boy."

"We can't afford to lose him."

"What we can't afford, Fred, is an officer who isn't dependable."

"Because he hit a rough patch is no reason to threaten him with termination. We can't all be as by-the-book as you are."

"You're skating near the edge, Fred. I know you didn't think I deserved this job, but I'm your boss for another two years."

"The people of this county didn't elect you. The only reason you got the job was because the mayor decided we needed new blood in the department. Things were going okay before you came."

Mandy felt her control slipping away and she didn't like the sensation. She shouldn't be at odds with her staff. Ken obviously didn't feel he could confide in her. Fred, for all his faults, had more years on the force than she'd been alive and he didn't think she could handle the job.

What is this about, God? What are you trying to tell me?

Rising, Mandy came around to the front of her desk. Crossing her arms, she settled her hip against it. "Let's not quarrel, Fred. You have a point. Crime is up and I can't get a handle on it."

"Don't try to placate me."

"I'm not. I'm telling you I need your help. You've lived in Timber Wells a long time and I've been here less than a year, but we both have the best interest of this community at heart."

The scowl stayed on his face. "If that's true, you'll lay off Ken."

Donna came in as Fred walked out. She

glanced from his ramrod straight back to Mandy. "What's up with him?"

"You'll have to ask him. What do you need, Donna?"

"I found the file you were looking for. The one about the murder that Judy Bowen supposedly witnessed in Kansas City."

Mandy reached for it eagerly. "It's about time."

"Someone had misfiled it, but it wasn't me. Unlike some people who work here, I know how to put things in alphabetical order."

Mandy frowned as she opened the folder. "Is this it? Is this all they sent? This is only the responding officer's report. Where are the forensic reports, the witness interviews?"

"Maybe there weren't any."

"I don't believe that for a minute. It was a homicide. There has to be more."

Donna threw up her hands. "I'll check around. Maybe the rest of it got misplaced, too. It's bad enough I have to do my own work. Now I've got to double check everyone else's."

"Let me know when you find it. If you don't, have K.C. fax it all again."

Ten minutes later, Mandy's intercom came on. Donna said, "Sheriff, line one is Agent Riley of the KBI."

Mandy leaned forward in her seat and pressed the button. "Hey, Jed. Tell me something good."

"Sorry. I'm not going to be of help this time. No DNA, no prints on your meth lab timer."

"Of course not," she muttered as she clenched her teeth in frustration.

She was back to square one.

Garrett lifted the carrier from its car seat base and slipped it over his arm. He allowed himself a weary smile as he walked toward the house. Two days after the social worker's visit, his son was home.

The late afternoon sun cast long shadows across the ranch yard. Pigeons swooped across the darkening sky through the open hayloft doors to land on the beams inside the old barn. Their gentle cooing mixed with the whispering of the wind, the bawling of cows in the pasture and the rising tide of cicada songs in the long grass.

It was the time of day Garrett loved best. It was good that this was the way his son should first see the ranch.

He glanced down at Colin. Of course, he was sleeping and didn't see anything, but someday Garrett would tell him the story of how he arrived — in a secondhand car seat

— in a used beat-up truck — on the prettiest evening of the year.

Wiley padded down from the front porch to meet them. The dog sniffed the air and began dancing in excited circles around Garrett's boots.

At the porch steps, Garrett sat down with the carrier in his lap. "Be easy, Wiley."

Wiley, his body quivering with barely contained eagerness, crept forward until his nose touched the baby sleeping in the infant seat. His tongue flicked out for a quick lick before Garrett could stop him.

Garrett pushed the dog's muzzle aside. "No, don't be kissing the baby. That's a firm new rule. There'll be no bending it."

Wiley sat back on his haunches and tipped his head to one side as he regarded the new arrival.

"This is Colin," Garrett said. "You're gonna have to help me keep an eye on him."

How pathetic was that? Asking a dog for parenting assistance.

Garrett would have laughed if the whole thing didn't scare him half to death. Now that he had Colin to himself, he was tempted to drive back to the hospital and return the kid for a refund. Surely there was someone better suited to raising a baby than he was.

Maybe there was, but in his heart, Garrett knew he needed his son more than anyone in the world. There was no way he was giving up a part of himself.

"Besides, the medical center would probably keep the money I paid on your bill, anyway." Garrett lifted the infant seat and carried his son into the house.

"This is it. This is home. I know it's not much to look at, but it'll be something special one day. We gonna do it together."

In the corner of the living room, a large cardboard box rested against the wall. Garrett hadn't had time to put the new crib together before he left for the hospital that morning. Hopefully, the crib would go together quickly and he'd have his son sleeping snuggly in it in no time.

He deposited the carrier on the sofa. Colin began to whimper. Wiley whined and barked at the sound. Garrett checked his watch. It wasn't time for a feeding. Colin had a bottle before leaving the hospital only twenty minutes earlier.

Lifting the baby out of his seat, Garrett raised him to his shoulder and bounced him as he patted his back. "What's wrong, little buddy?"

He tried to recall what the nurses had told him about crying. "Hungry, messy pants, tired, sick."

The first two were easy enough to fix, but would he be able to tell if Colin was sick and not just fussy?

Garrett laid a hand on the baby's forehead. He felt hot, but too hot? What was too hot for a baby?

Somewhere he had information about taking a temperature. The nurse had provided pages of printed instructions. He must have left them in the truck.

He returned Colin to his infant seat, but that made his crying skyrocket in volume. Wiley jumped onto the sofa beside the baby and began whining.

Red-faced with flailing arms and kicking feet, Colin Bowen was making his displeasure known in no uncertain terms.

"I'll be back in a second, I promise." Hurrying to the truck, Garrett returned with the pamphlets and quickly found the one on baby health and temperature taking. By the time Garrett managed to find a thermometer and get Colin undressed enough to put it under his arm, his nerves were about shot from the noise level.

To Garrett's relief, his son's temp was normal, but he continued to cry. Picking him up again didn't help. Garrett paced the floor with him, feeling more inadequate than he'd ever felt in his life.

Mandy heard the baby crying the minute she killed the engine and opened the truck door. Lights blazed from every window on the ground floor of Garrett's house.

It had been a long day, but she had to know that Colin was doing okay before she called it a night. From what she could hear, he wasn't.

Mandy quickly climbed the porch steps. If Garrett was mistreating that child, she'd haul Colin out of his custody in a heartbeat.

At the front door, she raised her fist to knock, but stopped when she caught sight of Garrett through the bay window.

He had Colin up to his shoulder as he walked back and forth across the living room bouncing the baby. At the look of exhaustion on the man's face, her anger faded. Apparently, Colin was breaking in his father the hard way.

She knocked, then knocked a second time when it was clear Garrett couldn't hear her over the crying. Finally, she opened the door and walked inside.

Wiley was huddled under the kitchen table with his head on his paws, a look of confusion on his face. Mandy walked through the archway that connected the kitchen to where Garrett was pacing. When his gaze lit on her, all she saw was relief. He didn't even question why she was in his house.

"He won't stop crying. I've done everything. I've fed him. I've changed him. I've been holding him for two hours. Why won't he stop crying?"

Crossing the room, Mandy took the baby from him. Garrett sank into a chair beside the pieces of unassembled crib with a look of total dejection on his face.

Colin repeatedly rubbed his tear-stained face against her shoulder as he continued to cry. She said, "I think he's just tired."

"That makes two of us. I can't get his bed put together because every time I put him back in his infant seat, he starts screaming again."

"Then put a blanket on the floor for him." She gestured toward a fleece throw on the corner of the sofa.

"I can do that?" His uncertain tone made her grin.

"Of course."

Rising wearily, he spread the coverlet on the floor. Kneeling, Mandy laid Colin in the center. Still fussing, the baby worked himself into his favorite position. Mandy patted his back until his crying gave way to occasional sobs. Before long, he was sound asleep.

Garrett stared at her, a look of awe on his face. "I don't believe it."

"It's a new place, new faces. He was exhausted, but he didn't want to give in."

Sinking onto the sofa, Garrett rested his elbows on his knees. "How do you know so much about kids?"

"I babysat for everyone on our block when I was in high school. The Pritchards, the O'Brians, the Dixons had four kids under four. I made three bucks an hour and learned you don't give kids anything with sugar before you send them to bed and that sometimes they just need to cry themselves to sleep."

"If I offer to double that salary for tonight will I be guilty of bribing an officer of the law?"

He'd actually made a joke. She smiled in return. "Six bucks an hour. That's tempting. Lucky for you I left my handcuffs at the office."

Garrett knew he'd been right. Her smile made her more than pretty. It made her downright beautiful.

Even the bruises on her face couldn't detract from a beauty that was more than skin-deep. Her eyes sparkled in the lamp-light. Her hair, loose about her shoulders, caught and reflected the light with a dozen subtle highlights, the same palette of colors the prairie wove into the grasses in the fall.

It wasn't only that she was pretty. There was something special about her. Something that made him wish he knew about love and what it was like to be loved in return.

It was a foolish wish. Love was a thing that happened to ordinary people, not to the likes of him.

A faint blush tinted Mandy's face. She dropped her gaze to the baby and Garrett realized he'd been staring. She softly began to run her fingers through Colin's curls.

What would it be like to be touched so gently?

A longing, powerful in its intensity, caught and held him within its grasp. It stole his breath as he watched her hand feather through his son's hair. In his whole life, he couldn't remember anyone touching him with such kindness.

Wiley padded in from the kitchen and sat near Garrett's boot. Yawning widely, the dog reminded Garrett of his own lack of sleep. He was bone-tired. Maybe that was why he was being so illogical.

He pushed up off the sofa. "I should get

back to work on the crib before he wakes up again."

Looking at the pieces spread around the room, she said, "It can't be that hard. Where are the directions?"

"I can usually figure things out on my own."

"If that isn't just like a man!" She rose to her feet. "Let me see them. This will go faster if we both work on it. I don't want Colin spending the night on the floor."

It was plain she was used to bossing people around. Garrett picked up the booklet but didn't give it to her. "I don't need help."

She held out her hand. "Put your wounded male ego aside and give me the instructions."

He surrendered the papers. "Trust me, they don't make sense."

Leafing through the diagrams, she opened to a center page. "They do if you read the ones in English."

"You'll think it's Japanese by step four."

Thirty minutes later, Mandy was kneeling beside him, an edge of exasperation in her tone. "It says slot F goes into slot D, right? This is F. This is D. Why don't they fit?"

Garrett sat back on his heels and tapped the handle of his screwdriver against his thigh. "Because we did something wrong."

"We didn't do anything wrong. We followed the directions exactly. I'm a college-educated woman, I should be able to put together a crib."

"Then the directions are wrong."

"That's not likely."

Wearily rising to his feet, he took a step back. "Then we're overlooking something."

She stood beside him, her hands fisted on her hips. "What?"

He studied the collection of parts on the floor. Realization dawned as he saw the tip on one wooden leg lying under the edge of the box. "Okay, I see it."

"What? Where?"

He pulled the piece from the pile of parts. "This is part F. The one we have is part C."

"Are you sure?" She snatched the instruction book from him and stared at the drawing. The pieces were similar, but he was right.

"Sometimes, it helps to take a step back and look at the whole picture," he said with a small grin.

Mandy slanted a glance his way. It was good advice for more than crib assembly. Had she been letting her own guilt, fears and suspicions color her perception of the man? If she took a step back and looked at him anew, what would she see?

Besides an attractive man, she saw callused hands used to rough work. She saw a man who didn't smile easily or trust easily. A man used to a solitary life, but who was willing to turn that life upside-down to take in a son he'd only just learned about.

There were a lot of things to like about Garrett Bowen, but one nagging question remained unanswered. His ex-wife, who may have known him better than anyone, didn't want him raising their child. Why not?

What did Judy know, or fear, about Garrett that made her decide strangers were better suited to raise her child? Mandy liked answers, not questions.

Grabbing the right part, Garrett fitted the pieces together and grinned at her when they fit perfectly. "It should go faster now."

Twenty minutes later they laid the bare mattress on the springs and stepped back. Mandy checked the front rail. It latched securely in each position and slid up and down easily. "It works."

"We should test it before we put Colin in it." Garrett's eyes lit on Wiley sitting beside Colin on the blanket. He snapped his fingers and the dog hurried over, his tail wagging.

Garrett lifted him into the crib and pulled

up the side. "He weighs more than Colin. If it holds him, it'll hold the baby."

Wiley clearly didn't enjoy being locked in. Quick as a wink, he leaped to the top of the rail and jumped out. Scampering back to the blanket, he dropped to his belly beside his charge.

Mandy giggled. "Hopefully, it will be a while before Colin learns to do that."

"No kidding."

"Do you have sheets?"

"Yeah." He left the room and returned with a pale blue fitted cotton sheet. Mandy was pleased to see he'd already washed it. It proved he'd made more than cursory preparations for Colin's arrival.

As he covered the mattress, Mandy glanced down at Wiley. "What's with that dog's tail?"

"The vet said it healed wrong after it was broken."

"How'd he break it?"

Garrett turned to face her. "I don't know. It happened before I found him."

She crouched beside the dog to scratch his head. "Poor boy. Where did you find him?"

"He was scavenging for scraps outside a sale barn in Tulsa. He looked kinda down on his luck. A couple of cowboys said he'd been hanging around for a few weeks. I gave him the rest of my cheeseburger and when I came out of the sale, he was waiting for me."

At the mention of food, Mandy's stomach growled loudly. She pressed a hand to her midsection. "A cheeseburger sounds good about now. I didn't have lunch."

Wiley exploded into the air, yipping wildly. Mandy jerked away in surprise, lost her balance and toppled backward.

"Wiley, quiet." At the command from Garrett, the dog settled on his haunches, an eager expression remaining on his face. Colin fussed for a second, then went back to sleep.

Extending a hand, Garrett helped Mandy to her feet. He pulled her up easily, proving he was every bit as strong as he looked.

Unexpected warmth surged up her arm at his touch. Her eyes met his. Their gazes locked. An arc of awareness passed between them.

He felt it, too. She read it on his face before his odd blank look replaced it.

Mandy pulled her hand away. Just when she thought she was beginning to understand him, he retreated where she couldn't follow.

"Sorry about the dog." He spoke to a spot just over her head. "He goes nuts when he hears it's mealtime. He didn't mean any harm."

She dusted off her jeans. "No harm done. I've got plenty of padding back there."

His gaze shifted to her face. The hollow look in his eyes gradually faded.

Mandy held up one finger. "Agree with that statement and you'll find yourself under arrest."

A ghost of a smile lifted the corner of his mouth. "Then I'd better exercise my right to remain silent."

"Excellent plan."

An awkward moment filled the space between them. Mandy used it to glance at her watch. "I should get going. It's getting late."

"Let me put this little fellow in his new digs, and I'll walk you out."

Tenderly, he picked up Colin, cuddling him against his chest briefly before transferring him into the crib. Wiley settled himself on the floor under the bed.

Mandy moved to stand beside Garrett. She laid a hand on Colin's head. She'd grown terribly fond of him. She wasn't quite sure how she was going to cope without visiting him every night at the hospital, without rocking him to sleep before returning to her own quiet, empty house.

Softly, she whispered, "Now I lay me down to sleep. I pray the Lord my soul to keep. May angels watch me through the night and keep me safe till morning's light."

She cleared her throat, knowing Garrett had heard the catch in her voice. With one last pat on Colin's back, she turned and headed for the door.

Outside on the porch, she stopped to fish her keys out of her pocket. Beside her, Garrett said, "I know you stopped in tonight to make sure Colin was okay because you were worried about him being with me."

"I was concerned about you, too." It wasn't a total falsehood. She had wondered how he was coping. She felt a blush creep up her neck and was glad the darkness hid it.

"My son is safe here, Sheriff. In spite of what you think, I'd never hurt him, and I didn't kill his mother."

Whatever closeness they'd shared slipped away. Mandy was back to being a cop.

"It's my job to be concerned about the people of this county. All of them, not just Colin. But for what it's worth, I don't think you'd harm him."

"You just think I killed his mother."

She studied his face in the porch light. "No. I don't believe you did."

The defiance on his features changed to stunned surprise. Turning away, Mandy walked out to her truck.

Glancing up at the starry heavens, she prayed, *Let me be right, Lord. For Colin's sake, let me be right this time.*

EIGHT

Friday was Mandy's morning off and she was ready for it. Although she normally worked Monday through Friday, once a month she covered a weekend evening shift to give her part-time staff a break.

The week so far had been a busy one with two new thefts of fertilizer from outlying farms and a burglary in town.

The break-in had been solved when she arrested a pair of teenagers for reckless driving and found some of the stolen items in their car. They were both high. It was clear they'd been stealing for drug money, but neither was willing to name their supplier.

She'd failed to keep two more children safe.

Shaking off the depressing thought, she poured the last dollop of hazelnut creamer into her coffee and glanced around her kitchen. Her days off were normally reserved for the exciting things in her life. Like shopping, laundry and dusting.

It was almost more fun than a girl could stand.

Taking a sip of coffee, Mandy realized she could easily ignore the dust on the television. What she couldn't ignore was how often her thoughts turned to Garrett and Colin. The emotional attachment she'd developed for the baby seemed to be expanding to include his father.

That wasn't something she had expected. The rational part of her mind told her to steer clear of Garrett, but another part of her longed to know him better. She wasn't sure what to do. That was an uncomfortable and unfamiliar sensation.

No matter what she felt, she couldn't, wouldn't let those feelings interfere with her job.

By the time she finished her coffee, she'd convinced herself that she had a handle on her emotions as far as Garrett was concerned. She also came to the conclusion that dusting could wait. Food was her top priority.

Fifteen minutes later, she left her side of the duplex, shopping list in hand, with the intention of filling her frighteningly empty refrigerator and cupboards. On the way to the grocery store, she caught sight of a hand-lettered yard sale notice tacked to a telephone pole at the end of her block.

The words *baby clothes* jumped out at her from the list of items being offered.

They probably won't have anything in Colin's size.

Still, what would it hurt to stop and look. It wasn't like the grocery story was going anywhere.

She turned left instead of right and that was how she ended up at a four-family garage sale on Maple Street with the cutest pair of blue bib overalls and a matching hat in Colin's size in her hands instead of fresh produce.

The outfit was simply too adorable to resist. She added it to the stack of equally precious infant outfits draped over her arm and resumed her search.

The sounds of small-town chitchat, laughter and occasional price haggling made her smile. Cars pulled up and stopped along the poplar-shaded street disgorging eager bargain hunters and simple browsers. It promised to be another warm day, but not unpleasant. It was, Mandy decided, small-town living at its best.

As long as her pager didn't go off, signaling she was needed for some emergency.

A pretty green sweater caught her eye just

as a white delivery van with a blue globe painted on the side double parked in the street, blocking traffic.

Mandy blew a strand of hair away from her face in mild exasperation. A clear traffic violation was taking place right in front of her.

To ticket or not to ticket, that was the question. She had her summons book in her truck.

Hopping down from his seat, the driver strolled to the first apartment with a white-and-blue box under his arm. The door opened and Donna Clareborn eagerly accepted her package.

Mandy smiled. No doubt her dispatcher, a self-proclaimed TV shopping addict, would be sporting a new purse or new shoes in church on Sunday.

The driver moseyed back to his vehicle, but instead of pulling away, he emerged with an additional package leaving his truck still double parked. He knocked at another apartment, but got no answer. Leaving the box propped against the door, he returned to his vehicle.

The flow of traffic was now at a standstill. An impatient driver began honking.

The woman who was running the sale added more items to an already-crowded

159

table beside Mandy and said, "You should give that jerk a ticket, Sheriff. He's always blocking my driveway."

Skeptical of what she assumed was an exaggeration, Mandy said, "I wouldn't think there would be *that* many deliveries. There are only ten units in the complex."

"Four or five times a week he parks right there and takes his own sweet time about it. Twice last week I was late picking up my kids from school because of him. I've even called the main office to complain, but it hasn't helped."

Mandy held out the clothes she'd picked up. "If you'll hold on to these for me, I'll go speak to him."

The deliveryman was certainly going to get a warning. She hadn't made up her mind about the ticket.

Walking across the street, Mandy noticed two teenagers loitering in the stairwell at the end of the complex. She recognized the redhead first. It was Luke Holt, Ken's younger brother. His buddy was one of the kids who'd heckled her during her speech at the high school. They saw her at the same time. They both turned and walked away with their heads down.

Little warning bells started going off in the back of Mandy's mind. She scanned the

160

area, but saw nothing else suspicious.

Meanwhile, the van driver stopped at an apartment several doors down from Donna's with a third parcel. Cedric Dobbs answered the knock. The principal grabbed the package out of the deliveryman's hands, then slammed the door in his face.

The driver shrugged and started toward his van. As he approached, Mandy reached for the badge in her hip pocket and held it up. The young man came to an abrupt halt, his eyes wide.

She said, "You do know it's illegal to park like that, don't you?"

"I'm sorry, Officer. I'm gonna move right now. Please, my boss will kill me if I get a ticket."

"I understand you make a lot of deliveries to this address."

"Yeah."

"Anything unusual about the packages you bring here?"

He scowled. "Unusual how?"

"That's what I'm asking."

"Look, Sheriff. I just deliver the stuff. I don't get nosy."

Another horn blast from behind the van convinced Mandy to send him on his way. "All right. Go, but don't let me see you blocking the street like this again."

"No, ma'am. Thank you." He jumped in his seat and drove away.

Mandy pulled her cell phone from her pocket and called the office. When one of the part-time dispatchers answered, Mandy said, "Who's on duty today?"

"Ken and Benny are both here."

"Let me talk to Benny."

When he came on the line, Mandy said, "I need you to do me a favor, Benny. Run a check on a delivery service called Global Shipping. See if anything odd pops up. I'll be in shortly, so leave anything you find on my desk."

After hanging up, Mandy returned to the yard sale and collected Colin's clothing from her grateful hostess.

Free to continue her shopping, Mandy happily browsed through stacks of second-hand goods and picked up another infant outfit she thought would be perfect for Colin.

Making her way around a tall garment rack filled with adult coats, she nearly tripped over a man crouched next to it examining a stroller. She only caught her balance by planting a hand on his shoulder. He looked up in surprise.

Mandy started to stutter an apology, but

gasped instead when she recognized Garrett.

Warmth that had nothing to do with the bright sunshine spiraled through her body and brought a blush to her face. Quickly she withdrew her hand and stepped back. "Excuse me. I wasn't watching where I was going."

As he rose, a flush crept up his neck and stained his chiseled cheeks a dull red. It appeared she wasn't the only one affected by the contact. The thought pleased her.

"Not a problem." He tipped his cowboy hat back with one finger then slipped his hands in his hip pockets.

For a long minute, they stood gazing at each other like two tongue-tied teenagers.

She looked away first, checking the area near him. "Where's Colin?"

"Ina Purdy is looking after him. She owns the ranch two miles south of me."

Mandy clutched her pile of clothing to her chest, trying not to look like she was dying for information about Colin and about Garrett. Nodding, she said, "I've had a few calls out to her place. The last time I was there, she promised she *wouldn't* vote for me in the next election."

To say Ina was eccentric was putting it mildly. Well over seventy and still running her own spread, the widow frequently clashed with the rancher whose place bordered hers to the west, her brother, Henry. The two constantly squabbled over straying cattle, Russian thistle control, poor fences and everything in between. Not a month went by that the office didn't get an irate call from Ina.

The barest smile tugged at the corner of Garrett's mouth. It changed his face from reserved to downright pleasant. "She's prickly, but she's been a good neighbor to me. She was the first one to hire me as her cattle buyer. She's taken a real shine to Colin."

That had to be the longest conversation Mandy ever heard from him. It seemed fatherhood was agreeing with him. "It's great that you have someone who can help. How are you and Colin getting along?"

"Good."

"No problems at all? Adjusting to a new baby in the house can be very stressful."

"I don't get as much sleep as I used to."

Frowning, she tipped her head to the side. "Isn't he sleeping through the night?"

"Colin is, but Wiley wakes me up every time the kid turns over. The mutt's a wreck."

Mandy chuckled. "You could banish him to the bathroom again."

"And separate him from Colin? Not a chance. He howls the house down when I try."

"It's hard to imagine Wiley in the role of a nanny."

"Almost as hard as imagining me in the role of Colin's father?"

"I'm coming to grips with that," she admitted.

Once again the silence lengthened. She struggled to find something to say that didn't sound inane.

Garrett rubbed the back of his neck. "I should get going. Mike Peters said he could weld a new hitch on my trailer if I got it over there this morning."

"It's a nice stroller, don't you think?" she said quickly before he could leave.

She wasn't sure *why* she didn't want him to leave. Maybe it was because she'd been feeling lonely and a little lost. She'd been attributing her slump to missing Colin and her late-night visits with him. But if she were being honest, she knew this stalling tactic wasn't about Colin. *This* was about Garrett.

He was becoming important to her. She wanted to peek behind the emotional wall he presented to the world.

Part of that was because he was Colin's

father, but part of it was because she found him intriguing and far too attractive for her peace of mind.

He nodded as he studied the stroller. "It looks like it's in good shape."

She turned her attention to the baby carriage. "It's got all the bells and whistles."

"Like what?"

She gripped the handle to demonstrate. "The sunshade comes up like this and if you push this button on the back, you can lay the seat down and make it into a bed."

"That's kinda slick."

"It has a place for carrying stuff underneath and it has a netting to keep the bugs off the baby. It even has a cup holder."

"So you think it's worth the money?"

"It's a name brand. You'd pay a lot more for it new."

"Guess I should take it. What treasures did you find?"

Don't be so delighted that he asked you a simple question.

But she was thrilled to share her finds. "I saw a couple of really cute outfits and I picked them up for Colin. They're only a dollar. Want to see them?"

"You don't have to buy clothes for him. I can take care of stuff like that."

Why did he have to be so touchy? Miffed,

she raised her chin. "I'm getting them for him because I want to. Would you like to see them or not?"

"Sure."

Mollified by his limited interest, she held up the first one. It was a light green sleeper with a yellow sailboat on it.

He hunched his shoulders forward. "Kinda girly, isn't it?"

"It is not girly." Offended, she laid it on the stroller handle and held up the next one. The overalls had blue and white checked cuffs and little metal buckles on the straps.

"I like that one," he admitted.

She grinned and held up a tiny white shirt with a red plaid vest, a matching bow tie and a pair of red pants. "Now, this one will be perfect for wearing to church."

Garrett didn't respond until she looked at him. He said, "Colin won't be going to church."

Mandy frowned. In her mind, attending worship was as natural as breathing. To imagine Colin would be raised without knowing God's love and mercy was deeply disturbing.

"How do you know what size to get him?" Garrett asked.

"Baby clothes sizes are based on age. Always get them a little big because he'll grow out of them in a hurry. May I ask why you don't plan to take Colin to church?"

"I don't go."

Prayers that Garrett would undergo a change of heart were definitely being added to her daily conversation with God. She folded the outfits as she debated a moment before voicing what she was thinking. "Maybe this isn't any of my business."

Garrett tipped his head toward her. "Has that ever stopped you before?"

She grinned. "No. As a matter of fact, it hasn't."

Once again Garrett found himself entranced by Mandy's smile. It was as fresh as a sun-drenched spring morning. He wouldn't mind basking in the glow for as long as she cared to bestow it.

She was out of uniform today. Casually dressed in a mint-green shirt over a matching tank top edged with lace and tan shorts, she looked carefree and happy. Like any other mother or wife enjoying a yard sale. Her hair was pulled back into a ponytail, but a few wisps danced at her temple when the wind teased them.

The bruises on her face were beginning to fade, but seeing them still caused him a pang of distress. She wasn't his to worry about, but he hated the idea that her job put her in danger.

Her smile slowly faded as she studied his face. Finally, she said, "Reverend Spencer mentioned it was important to Judy to have her child raised in a Christian home. He said her faith meant a lot to her at the end. Don't you think you should take her wishes into consideration?"

Garrett's euphoria evaporated. Her interest was in Colin, not in him. He had no business thinking anything else. Imagining she might care about him was a quick trip to heartache. A place he'd been too many times.

"I haven't given it much thought," he replied.

He didn't need Mandy reminding him that Judy thought he was unfit to raise his own son. He still didn't understand why she felt that way. With her dead, he probably never would.

Maybe she saw something in him that reminded her of her own abusive father. As hard as Garrett had tried to hide it from her, maybe Judy knew he was flawed inside and that was why she wanted to keep Colin away from him.

"Do you believe in God, Mr. Bowen?" Mandy was still watching him with those intense blue eyes that saw and catalogued every detail.

She would see it soon, too, his flawed soul. She'd uncover his cowardice. Then she'd look at him with pity or worse — with repugnance.

"I believed in God once."

"But not anymore?"

"You have a job that deals with the dirty, cruel side of people. Why do you still believe in God?"

"Because for every evil thing that men do, a hundred men do the right thing. Good things. Why? Because God gave us a free will. God is like a loving father. He *is* a loving father. He's always with us no matter how hard life is."

"Not every father is loving, Sheriff."

"Sadly, that's true. We live in an imperfect world. Cruelty, poverty, disease, they all exist and they always will."

"I thought you were arguing in favor of God's existence."

"I am. No matter what afflicts us, God's love is there to help us bear it. That's what gets me through the hard days."

There had been a time when he'd wanted, needed God in his life, but God had been busy elsewhere.

"I get myself through the hard days," he

said with a conviction he didn't feel.

"I guess that is my point," Mandy said. "You don't have to do it alone. Our Lord was asked which was the greatest commandment. He replied, 'Love the Lord your God with all your heart and with all your soul and with all your mind. This is the first and greatest commandment. And the second is like it: 'Love your neighbor as yourself.'

"Church isn't just about worshipping God. It's also about caring for each other."

Garrett fought the pull of her words. To depend on someone. To be loved and cared for by someone. Did she even know what she was offering? How could she? She had no idea what it was like to be alone — to pray for help that never came.

Garrett turned away before she read in his eyes how much he wanted to believe in what she said. Folding up the stroller, he tucked it under his arm. "Is there anything new on Judy's murder?"

"No. Nothing new."

"Thanks for everything you've done so far."

"I wish it could have been more."

That he did believe. With a nod in her direction, he crossed the lawn to the table where the woman with the cash box sat, paid for his purchase and left.

Mandy watched him drive away, then looked down at the clothes she held. She could have given them to Garrett to take home, but she hadn't. Now, she'd have to drive out and deliver them in person.

As an excuse to see Colin, it might be a bit lame. Just so as long as Garrett didn't think it was an excuse to see *him* again.

Even if it was.

He claimed he didn't need help, but she sensed a loneliness about him that drew her to him as she'd never been drawn to another man.

Had anything she said about faith gotten through to him? Colin deserved to grow up knowing God.

Mandy was willing to let the subject drop for now, but not for long. She paid for the baby clothes in her hands and walked to her truck.

After leaving the yard sale, she had just enough time left to stop at the market and pick up her groceries before she headed home to change.

An hour later, she entered the office to find Benny laying a sheet of paper on her desk. He said, "Here's the information you asked for on Global Shipping."

"Anything interesting?" She picked up the

paper and gave it a quick scan.

"Not much. It's a small operation based out of Wichita. Can I ask why you're interested?"

"Someone mentioned this company had been making a lot of deliveries to the apartment complex on Maple Street. Maybe it's nothing, but I thought I'd look into it."

"You don't really think someone's shipping meth in or out of town in delivery vans, do you?"

Mandy shook her head as she laid the paper on her desk. "At this point, I'm not ruling out anything. I'm willing to start pulling over carrier pigeons."

Benny chuckled. "Good luck with that. What's the plan for this afternoon?"

"I think I'll go out on patrol. I don't feel like doing paperwork today."

Rolling his eyes, Benny said, "Who does?"

Fifteen minutes later, Mandy was cruising down the highway toward the eastern county line. As mile after mile of pastures and farmland slid past, she found herself lulled into a sense of calm. She loved the peace and sense of belonging she'd found among these rolling hills and green countryside. More than ever, she was determined to root out the scum that threatened the people who lived here.

With Your help, Lord, I know it's possible.

She'd gone about ten miles when she first noticed the semi truck behind her. It was a black rig with a bright chrome grill that glinted in the sunlight and it was coming up fast.

Truckers normally slowed when they saw her vehicle. This one didn't. He kept coming, closing the gap between them.

Mandy glanced at her speedometer. She was doing the speed limit. When she checked her rearview mirror again, the semi was blowing past her. It was a cattle hauler.

As the gray, hole-filled trailer pulled alongside, she could see it was empty. Whatever the reason for his rush was, it wasn't because he had a load to deliver. She flipped on her lights and siren.

Okay, buddy, you're going to get a ticket.

She barely had time to form the thought before she felt the impact as the trailer swung back and sideswiped her. Her SUV veered off the road into the shallow ditch. Mandy fought to keep control as she bounced over the grassy sod and tore through a barbed-wire fence. She gripped the wheel with white-knuckled strength.

Finally, she managed to come to a stop. Her heart hammered in her chest as she drew a shaky breath.

The semi hadn't even slowed down.

He was not getting away with this!

Her tires spun as she jammed her foot on the accelerator and drove back through the broken fence and onto the blacktop.

She grabbed her radio mic as she headed after her quarry. "Dispatch, this is Sheriff Scott. I'm in pursuit of a hit-and-run tractor-trailer heading east on Highway 56 nearing the Bushong turnoff. Patch me through to the Highway Patrol. I'm gonna need some help stopping this guy."

"Copy that." It was Ken's voice. "Benny's on his way to you now."

Gaining on the truck, Mandy quickly relayed information on the make and tag number to the Highway Patrol. Without a unit in her area, the best they could do was to set up a roadblock farther down the highway.

Hanging back, she kept the vehicle in sight, but didn't try to stop it. One sideswipe had been enough. He could plainly see her red lights and hear her siren. It was clear he had no intention of stopping.

Suddenly, the truck ahead of her slammed on its brakes and tried to turn onto a county road. He didn't make it. Jackknifing, the weight of the trailer pushed the cab into the ditch in a cloud of dust.

175

Mandy quickly stopped and reported her location. She tried to get out, but her smashed door was jammed. She had to scramble across the seat to the passenger's side.

A man in a red T-shirt, jeans and a dark ball cap jumped out of the cab and took off across the field toward a stand of trees before she could get out. Thrusting open the door, she jumped out and drew her gun. A second man stumbled out of the rig with his hands in the air. He sank to his knees.

"Get on the ground. Hands behind your back," she yelled at him. When he complied, she quickly cuffed him.

"It was an accident," he snarled.

"Save it," she muttered as she checked for weapons. Finding none, she hauled her captive to his feet and pushed him toward her vehicle.

One look at her smashed rear door and broken window made it clear she couldn't leave him in the Bronco while she pursued his buddy.

Blowing out a breath of pure frustration, she began to read him his rights while she waited for backup to arrive.

Five minutes later, Benny came speeding down the highway and screeched to a halt in his cruiser. Jumping out he hurried toward her. "Are you all right?"

"I'm fine."

Mandy pushed her prisoner toward him. "Keep this one and take his statement. I'm going after the driver."

Benny grabbed the man's arm and shoved him toward the car. "I'll take care of him."

Nodding her thanks, Mandy took off at a lope, following the trail of crushed grass through the knee-high blue stem until she reached the edge of the woods.

Stepping under the thick canopy of hackberry, oak and walnut trees hugging the edge of a tiny creek, Mandy crouched to make herself a smaller target and paused to listen. She heard nothing but the sounds of birds, insects and her own breathing.

The damp ground was littered with decomposing leaves and fallen limbs. Thick clumps of grass and thorny bushes were scattered throughout the grove wherever enough light filtered in to sustain them.

She studied the ground and quickly spotted the direction her quarry had taken. Hoping she could save herself the trouble of tramping through the thorn bushes, she called out. "This is the Morrison County sheriff. Come out with your hands where I can see them."

No response.

Of course not. Why didn't they ever make it easy?

Moving forward but keeping an eye out for an ambush, Mandy pressed deeper into the timber and followed the course of the creek.

She knew the area. A quarter of a mile ahead, the waterway fed out into a pond in a pasture. After that, the only cover her fugitive would have would be grass and the occasional cow for the next two miles.

The man in front of her had four options. Fight, give up, hide in this strip of trees or try and circle back to the highway and flag down a ride. How smart was he? How desperate?

She had to assume the worst.

Fallen leaves and twigs crackled underfoot as she moved forward. The wind had all the trees in motion, causing shadows to dance and limbs to creak.

She lost the trail once, but picked it up again where he'd slid down the bank into the water and scrambled up the other side. Mandy followed. The water was only ankle deep; it didn't slow her down but pulling herself up the far bank did.

She holstered her gun. Grabbing a pair of protruding roots, she hauled herself up, scrambling for toeholds with her boots. She finally gained enough purchase to hoist herself up and over.

He was waiting for her.

She had a split second to throw herself to the side as he swung a hefty club. It thudded into the dirt beside her head.

Latching on to the wood with one arm to keep him from swinging again, Mandy kicked out hard, catching him in the knee. He grunted in pain but didn't go down. Twisting the club out of her grasp, he raised it again. Mandy rolled away and surged to her feet, her hand going to her holster. It was empty.

Startled, she looked down. The gun had fallen out and lay between them in the leaves.

Her attacker grinned as he advanced a step. Mandy judged the distance to her firearm, calculating her chances of getting to it before he struck. She took a step to the left. He raised the limb overhead and rushed at her.

Ducking low, she threw herself into his midsection in a flying tackle. They both went down. Scrambling away from him, she reached for her gun, but he gabbed her leg and pulled her back.

Rolling over, Mandy kicked his face with her free foot. His head snapped back and his grip loosened. She launched herself at her weapon and felt her fingers close over the familiar grip.

Surging to her feet, she leveled her gun at him. "Hold it right there."

He had regained his feet, but there was blood pouring from his nose. Rage filled his eyes. Raising the barrel a fraction so he could look into it, she said, "Think you're faster than a speeding bullet? Go ahead and try."

Slowly the fight drained out of him. He raised his hands.

"Good choice. Turn around and start walking toward the highway."

Staying a few steps behind him, Mandy followed, her gun trained on his back. After they'd covered a hundred yards, Mandy heard Benny calling her name. She answered and in another minute he appeared through the trees.

He grinned from ear to ear when he caught sight of her. "I see you found your stray. Are you okay?"

"Yeah."

"Highway Patrol just arrived."

"Better late than never."

Pulling her suspect's hands behind his back, Benny slapped on his pair of hand-cuffs. Eyeing the suspect's bloody face,

Benny said, "Looks like he gave you some trouble."

"He tried to walk softly and carry a big stick, but I followed my dad's advice."

"What was that?"

"Forget the stick. Use a gun."

After her prisoner had been Mirandized, Mandy guided him to Benny's squad car. Depositing him with his buddy, she closed the door, then leaned against the rear fender as the draining adrenaline left her feeling weak-kneed and shaken.

Benny, hands on his hips, still had a smile on his face. Some guys just liked the rush.

The highway patrol officer, who had been searching the inside of the truck cab, came over to Mandy. He held up a large thermos. "Nice work, Sheriff. This is quite a haul."

She raised an eyebrow. "You want to bust them for bad coffee?"

The trooper didn't even crack a smile. Unscrewing the lid, he shook some of the contents into it and held it toward her.

Stepping closer, Mandy saw a dozen small plastic bags filled with pink crystals. "Meth!"

"There are six more of these inside the cab. You're looking at a street value of close to twenty thousand dollars here."

"Wow." Benny strode toward the cab.

Mandy glanced toward the prisoners in the back of the squad car. "That explains why they tried to run, but it doesn't explain why they tried to kill me."

The officer replaced the cap of the thermos. "According to your first suspect, it was an accident. When they realized they'd hit a police car, they panicked."

Mandy shook her head. "I don't buy it."

"The truck belongs to a firm in Oklahoma City. We're running your suspects' licenses now. From their log, it appears they were on their way to pick up a load of cattle from a ranch near Kansas City."

Mandy raked her hands through her hair, pulling out several clinging twigs. "The real question is, where did they stop for coffee?"

A big score of meth had been on its way to Kansas City via her county. Her instincts said it was no coincidence, but she needed proof.

She walked toward the cab. "Benny, I want the whole cab dusted for prints. See if you can track where this rig has traveled in the past twenty-four hours. Look for receipts, fast food trash, anything that will tell us where they've been. I'm not trusting their log books."

Benny, sitting in the driver's seat, bent forward and pulled a clipboard full of papers toward him. Looking down at her, he said, "I can tell you one place they stopped."

"Where?"

He handed the clipboard to her. "They fueled up in Timber Wells less than an hour ago."

NINE

Garrett stood inside the convenience area of Turner's as he waited for Mike to finish welding a bigger hitch on the back of his pickup. The rank odors of old coffee, pine cleaner and the occasional whiff of gasoline from the pumps outside made him wish Mike would hurry up.

Once his truck was finished, he'd be able to pick up the larger, secondhand stock trailer he had purchased the week before. Currently, he had to split his commission with another hauler when his orders were too big for the small trailer he owned. This way, he could haul more cattle and keep more of his profits in his own pockets.

He shifted from one foot to the other as he waited and watched through the window. Mike, in a welding helmet and gloves, worked at the back of Garrett's truck amid a shower of sparks. Two big rigs sat idling in a parking area behind the building. There was nothing unusual in the sight. The truck stop always did a booming business.

Garrett glanced toward the four red vinyl booths at the back of the room. A pair of rough-looking characters occupied the last booth. Sporting black ball caps and black T-shirts with grinning skulls, both men were red-eyed, hollow-cheeked and unshaven.

Garrett recognized the tall one as Spike Carver. Judy and Spike had moved in the same unsavory circles when she was doing drugs. Garrett didn't know the smaller man.

Spike's buddy shook a pill into his palm from a small vial and popped it in his mouth. He offered the vial to Spike, but Spike pushed his hand aside. "Cool it, J. J."

Spike had noticed Garrett watching them. J. J. followed his gaze. The pit bull glare he leveled at Garrett was pure malice. It was clear J. J. was amped up on speed and spoiling for a fight.

Spike, on the other hand, was nervous as a cat, glancing about frequently in a paranoid fashion.

Garrett turned his back on them. He didn't want trouble with a couple of junkies. Picking up a copy of *Kansas Ranch,* he began to leaf through it.

The bell over the door jangled. Garrett glanced that way just as Mandy walked in.

She was dressed in her uniform, but it was grimy and stained.

Pulling off her sunglasses, she hooked one earpiece in her shirt pocket and surveyed the room. Her eyes settled on Garrett for a long second, then moved to the man behind the counter. She looked like a woman on a mission.

Aaron Turner frowned and leaned his forearms on the countertop. "Sheriff Scott, what happened to you?"

"A minor scuffle. You should see the other guy. I need to ask you a few questions about a cattle hauler that was here this morning."

From the corner of his eye, Garrett saw the men in the booth tense. They exchanged pointed, wide-eyed glances. J. J. leaned down and slipped something from his boot. Garrett caught the glint of a knife blade as the man transferred it to his pants pocket.

At the counter, Aaron said, "A lot of cattle trucks stop here. Could you be more specific?"

"Yellow Weaver cab, potbelly trailer, Oklahoma tags." Mandy, intent on describing the vehicle, appeared not to notice as Spike and J. J. slid out of their booth.

Aaron straightened and spread his hands wide. "I don't recall it. Sorry."

"They have a receipt for diesel fuel from

186

your pump time-stamped eleven thirty-five today."

His eyebrows rose a fraction. "They do? Then they must have been here. Are they in some kind of trouble? Has there been an accident?"

"I need to know if they spoke to anyone or met with anyone while they were here."

Aaron rubbed his jaw. "Let me get Mike. I think he was manning the counter then. Maybe he can be more helpful."

Spike and his buddy moved past Garrett as they headed for the front door where Mandy stood with her back to them. Both men pulled their hats low and kept their heads down.

Garrett's breath froze in his lungs. The need to protect Mandy rushed in, blocking any other thought from his mind.

Rolling his magazine into a tight cylinder, Garrett brushed past them deliberately bumping into J. J. as he put himself between the men and Mandy.

"Watch where you're going," J. J. snarled.

Aaron said loudly, "Sheriff, why don't we look through our receipts and see if there were other sales made around the same time. It might jog my memory."

In the curved mirror on the wall, Garrett could see Mandy moving in their direction.

Spike pulled on his buddy's arm. "Let's get out of here."

"Not until this clodhopper says he's sorry."

"Is there a problem?" Mandy stood at the end of the aisle watching them with narrowed eyes.

Spike rubbed one hand over the stubble on his chin. "No problem, Sheriff."

She took a step closer. "Hello, Spike. Hello, J. J. You two been here long?"

"All morning," J. J. answered quickly, then looked down as he shifted from one foot to the other.

Garrett tensed as J. J. slipped his hand into the pocket of his baggy pants.

"Be cool, J. J.," Spike cautioned in a harsh whisper.

Mandy took a step closer. "In that case, I've got some questions for you. What do you know about a shipment of meth that left here an hour ago?"

J. J.'s eyes went wide. He pulled his knife, but Garrett brought the rolled magazine down hard on his wrist. The four-inch blade clattered to the floor.

Mandy advanced with her gun drawn. "Hands up, all of you!"

J. J. clutched his wrist, muttering curses under his breath.

Spike raised his hands quickly. "I'm not armed. I had no idea he was."

Mandy motioned to Garrett with a jerk of her head. "Step away from the knife."

He backed up a pace. In retrospect, it had been a really stupid move on his part. She was armed with a gun and trained to take care of herself in dangerous situations. He had a rolled-up copy of *Kansas Ranch*. All he would have needed to do was to call out a warning.

Only none of that occurred to him when he saw she was in danger. He'd been driven to protect her.

Because he cared about her.

The thought caught him broadside with its intensity. She was the last woman he should be interested in. She thought he'd murdered his ex-wife. She could prevent him from keeping custody of his son.

He was a no-account cowboy eking a living out of a rundown spread. She was one of the most respected women in the county. She hadn't looked at him twice until he became a suspect in Judy's murder.

They had nothing in common.

So they'd spent a few minutes talking politely over a stroller that morning. It was hardly a sign she'd welcome his attention. Even dreaming about something between them was as foolhardy as facing a man with a knife.

Spike, his hands still raised, said, "I didn't do nothing. I didn't know he had a knife."

Mandy's gun didn't waver. "Back up against the wall and sit down with your legs straight out in front of you and your hands on your head. You, too, Garrett."

So much for her being grateful for his help. He and Spike did as she instructed. Within moments, she had J. J. in handcuffs, had called for backup, read him his rights and then began searching him.

When she pulled the brown vial from his pocket, she smiled. "Look what I found."

"That's not mine." J. J.'s gaze darted to Spike.

"No? Who does it belong to?" she asked.

J. J. nodded toward Garrett. "That cowboy must have slipped it in my pocket."

"That's right." Spike spoke up quickly. "He bumped into J. J. as soon as he saw you come in. He was getting rid of the evidence."

Garrett tensed. Would she believe them? Or would he be arrested again for something he hadn't done?

Had his desire to protect Mandy just cost him his son and his freedom?

■ ■ ■ ■

Mandy watched as a shuttered look dropped over Garrett's face. Until that moment, she didn't think he'd been involved, but now she wasn't so sure. Reading Garrett was like trying to navigate by the stars on an overcast night. Not easy.

She clapped a hand on J. J.'s the shoulder. "If that's the case, then you won't mind taking a drug test, will you?"

He seemed to shrink before her eyes. He was going to test positive and he knew it.

The bell of the door jangled and Mike walked inside. He glanced from Mandy to his partner who was still behind the counter. "What's going on?"

Aaron shrugged. "I think it's a simple misunderstanding."

"Not so simple," Mandy replied. "One of your tow truck drivers pulled a knife on me."

Mike slapped his welding gloves against his thigh. "Then he's fired. Bowen, your truck is done."

"What?" J. J. squawked. "Bowen gets away with murdering his ex-wife and you're gonna fire me for having a pocket knife? Where's the justice in that?"

J. J. continued whining until the backup Mandy had called for walked in the door. She turned her prisoner and the evidence over to her deputy, then came back to stand in front of Spike and Garrett.

She made each of them stand in turn and face the wall while she searched them. Finding nothing, she stepped back and said, "I could hold both of you as material witnesses and maybe as accessories, but I'm not in the mood for more paperwork today."

Garrett relaxed when he realized she wasn't going to lock him up.

"Let me make this clear," she continued. "I won't tolerate meth in my town. If you're involved, you'll find yourself behind bars. Do I make myself clear?"

Spike settled his cap on his head. "Clear as a bell, Sheriff."

As he left the building, Mandy looked at Garrett. "You can go, too."

"Yes, ma'am." He started toward the door, but she called after him.

"Garrett, I know you meant well, but next time don't interfere like that. You could have gotten hurt. I can take care of myself."

He stopped, but he didn't look back or answer her. After a long moment, he walked out the door.

■ ■ ■ ■

An odd sense of loss came over Mandy as she stared after him. She couldn't decide if Garrett was foolish, brave, a criminal — or all three.

After finishing her interview with Aaron and his tightlipped partner, she didn't find much that was useful.

While she didn't care for either of the station owners, Aaron had at least been helpful. The receipts had jogged his memory into putting her suspects in conversation with an out-of-town customer who bought gas, a soda and some chips when the men she'd arrested had also been in the store. They could have met outside without being seen.

Aaron's description of the man had been vague to the point of being almost useless. A white male, thirty to forty years old, wearing a dark cowboy hat. Mandy's hopes that the video surveillance would yield better information had been dashed when she learned the cameras were only for show. They'd never been hooked up. The partners thought their presence was enough to deter people from driving away without paying.

Mike couldn't recall anything about the

truck or the other customers. Mandy wasn't sure if he honestly paid that little attention or if he just didn't like talking to a cop.

Despite coming up empty-handed at the gas station, Mandy had the satisfaction of knowing her office had taken a large shipment of meth out of circulation. Her hopes of uncovering a connection between her suspects and the drug manufacturer were now riding on the men in jail. She would ask Tom Wick to offer them a deal in exchange for information.

It wasn't the best solution, but it might be the only way to catch bigger fish.

When she was done at Turner's, she drove back to the office. Her plan was to let J. J. and the truck drivers stew for a while. She was sure there was a connection between the three men. It was just a little too coincidental that J. J., a known user, had been at the truck stop at the same time.

J. J. was a small-time crook. He'd been arrested for petty crimes a couple of times in the past year. She didn't believe for a minute that he was the brains behind the operation she was battling, but he could well be a cook or distributor.

If she could get the county attorney to agree to cut J. J. a deal on his possession and weapons charges today, he just might roll over and give her the names she needed.

Fred was at his desk when she walked in. She didn't pause as she headed toward her office. "Have J. J. Fields taken to the interrogation room. I want to have a word with him."

"It won't do you any good."

Mandy spun around. "What do you mean?"

"All three of your prisoners have lawyered up and are refusing to talk."

"Are you serious? How did their lawyers get here so fast?"

"Both attorneys were already at the courthouse on other cases this morning."

Pressing her fingertips to her suddenly throbbing temples, Mandy sighed. She would go ahead with the plan to offer the men deals, but she had hoped to be able to question them first. "We can't catch a break."

Fred said, "J. J. was yelling that Garrett Bowen was the one who slipped the meth in his pocket. Seems like a big coincidence that he was at Turner's at the same time that your drug mules stopped there. How come you didn't bring him in for questioning?"

Glancing at him sharply, she noticed he was alone. "Where's Donna?"

"I sent her out for some lunch. She should be back soon. You didn't answer my question."

"I didn't bring Garrett in because he tried to protect me when J. J. pulled a knife. Besides, he was with me at eleven thirty."

Fred's eyebrows shot up. "Is that so? Still, that doesn't mean he didn't meet those men before they pulled out of Tucker's."

She'd already considered the possibility. She just didn't want to accept it.

"I'll be in my office for the next hour or so. Put through any calls that come in about the arrests this morning. I might as well get some paperwork done while I wait to hear if the KHP comes up with anything else on those truckers."

The next two hours of Mandy's day was spent filling out paperwork and running down leads with the KHP. According to the highway patrol, the Tulsa trucking company seemed to be legit, as did the rancher shipping the cattle on the other end. The KHP, like her office, simply didn't have much to go on. It would take a couple of days to process the evidence in the truck. Hopefully, that would offer some new leads.

By the end of a long and frustrating day, she was ready to go home and take a well-deserved soak in a steaming hot bath.

She did just that, but neither the honeysuckle-scented bubble bath nor the lavender-scented candles she liked so well eased the restlessness that plagued her.

Rather than pace the small floor of her living room, Mandy got dressed again and headed for the door. On the way out, she scooped up the clothes she'd purchased for Colin.

Had it really only been that morning? It felt like years had passed.

Within minutes, she was driving down the highway toward Garrett's ranch. She simply couldn't get the man out of her mind. He was such a contradiction. One minute he'd been sweet and kind, talking with her about baby equipment, God and Wiley's neurotic behavior. The next time she'd seen him, he'd been picking a fight with J. J. and Spike. What was up with that?

Had it been for her benefit or had it been designed to throw her off the track by making it *look* as if he wasn't involved with them?

She wished she knew.

To her surprise, Garrett's house was dark when she drove into the yard, but lights shone from the small square windows of the barn and spilled out of the open doorway in a broad rectangle.

Sitting off to the side of the barn was an older model black Ford pickup truck.

Black, like the one that had forced Judy Bowen off the road.

An ugly suspicion popped into Mandy's head. Who was the owner? What were they doing in Garrett's barn at this time of night?

Slipping out of her Bronco, she closed the door quietly. If they hadn't already been alerted to her presence, so much the better. Unsnapping the flap of her holster, she cautiously approached the truck to check the front end. Even in the poor light she could see it wasn't damaged.

She relaxed slightly until the murmur of voices from inside the building reached her. One of them belonged to a woman.

"You're too soft, Garrett. Put the little thing out of his misery."

"I will if I have to, but I'm not giving up yet."

Mandy walked inside, her boots making almost no sound on the soft dirt floor. The interior of the barn smelled of animals and hay and old wood. She followed the sound of the voices to the very back of the building.

"Suit yourself," the woman said. "It's not like you don't already have enough on your plate."

"I'm managing."

Mandy approached the gray-haired woman leaning on the door of a straw-filled stall. There was a stroller near her feet. Garrett sat in the middle of the stall with a tiny black calf in his lap, trying to get it to take an oversized bottle with a red rubber nipple.

Mandy quietly snapped the flap of her holster closed. No drug ring, no meth lab or murder plots being hatched. Just a weary-looking rancher, trying to save one small animal.

So much for her suspicious mind. Sometimes, it was a curse, as well as a blessing.

Pasting a smile on her face, she stepped close to the gray-haired woman. "What's going on here?"

The elderly lady spun around with a hand pressed to her chest. Mandy recognized her as Garrett's neighbor, Ina Purdy.

"Land sakes, girl. Don't go sneaking up on a body like that. You nearly gave me a heart attack."

"I'm sorry. I thought you heard me drive in."

Mandy saw Wiley sitting beside the stroller Garrett had purchased that morning. He trotted over to her and she stooped to pet him. Stepping close to the stroller, she saw

Colin was sound asleep and sucking his thumb.

"What are you doing here?" Garrett asked. He had that guarded look in his eyes again.

Don't admit you've been asking yourself that same question for the last ten minutes.

"I stopped by to drop off the clothes I bought for Colin at the yard sale. I meant to give them to you earlier, but I got . . . distracted. Hope you don't mind my dropping by. I guess I should have called."

"I think you stopped in to see if I've been letting Colin puff on my crack pipe."

She couldn't really blame him for his sarcasm.

"Why would the sheriff be interested in cracked pipes?" Ina scowled at both of them.

"Crack, crank, ice, speed, they're all names for meth," Garrett explained.

Ina looked ever-more puzzled. "That stuff's illegal. Sheriff, if you think this young man is doing something criminal, you've got bad instincts, and I'm *sure* not gonna vote for you come election time. 'Course, you're better than that lazy Fred Lindholm. He always takes my brother's side. Neither one of them have any respect for women. If you need someone to arrest, go haul in my worthless brother."

Mandy tried not to smile as she listened

to Ina's tirade. "On what charge?"

Ina slapped her hand on the wooden stall door. "Being mean and ugly, that's what for."

"My jail would be full before daybreak if I arrested every mean or ugly man in the county."

"That's the plain truth, but Garrett here wouldn't be one of them. He's a soft-hearted fool, that's what he is, and he didn't kill that ex-wife of his."

"The sheriff isn't interested in opinions, Ina. She needs proof," he muttered and began trying to feed the calf again.

Mandy hadn't expected Garrett to greet her with open arms, but she had hoped for a little warmer welcome.

She turned her attention to Colin. Dropping to her knees beside the baby, Mandy reached out and stroked his cheek. She'd missed him so much.

"Hey, little guy. I come all this way to see you and you're just gonna sleep? What kind of greeting is that?"

Garrett said, "He's had a long day."

"Me, too," Mandy admitted with a weary sigh.

Garrett continued to coax the tiny calf to eat, but when he glanced at Mandy, his gaze softened. "At least you got a few bad guys off the street today. That should make you happy."

"It does, actually, but they'll be out on bail in a few days, so I'm not gloating. J. J. is claiming the whole thing was a frame. I hope you are willing to testify as to what happened."

"I will."

"Thanks. A lot of people don't want to get involved when it comes to actually appearing in court."

"Don't blame them," Ina interjected. "There are more crooks who work in the courthouse than get arrested. And most of them were elected!"

Rising, Mandy opened the stall gate and stepped inside. Her boots sank deep into the fresh straw. "What seems to be the trouble with this little fellow?"

Ina didn't wait for Garrett to answer. "He was born prematurely. He wasn't meant to survive."

"His mother rejected him." The pain in Garrett's voice touched something deep inside Mandy. He knew exactly what that felt like. According to Fred, Garrett's mother had left him when he was a small boy.

Garrett tried again to get the calf to suckle on the bottle. It showed no interest, but bawled pitifully instead.

"Let me try." Mandy took the bottle from Garrett. Opening the lid, she dipped her fingers in the milk, then offered her hand to the calf.

Ina shook her head and gave them both a pitiful look. "Sheriff, I know you think I'm being cruel, but it's best to let nature take its course. He's too weak. There isn't any point in trying to save him."

Mandy met Garrett's eyes. "Maybe the point is to try, even if we don't succeed."

Ina sighed loudly and shook her head. "Fools rush in. I can tell when my opinion isn't wanted. I'm gonna take Colin up to the house. When you two figure out it's a lost cause, I'll be watching the late show."

As Ina wheeled Colin out of the barn, Mandy dipped her fingers into the milk again and pushed them inside the calf's mouth. It took a feeble suck. "That's it. Come on. You can do it."

"Ina's probably right. I think he's blind, too." Garrett waved his fingers in front of the calf's eyes. It didn't flinch.

Moving his hand back to the animal's side, he softly rubbed across the calf's shiny black coat in gentle strokes. The movement mesmerized Mandy.

He had such strong-looking hands. His

fingers were long and blunt with short, clean nails in spite of his outdoor life. She liked that about him.

Sitting next to him in the soft hay, listening to the sounds of the other cattle in the barn was comfortable in a way she'd never known with another man. She liked his gentleness, his determination to raise his son, even the way he kept a pretty much useless dog with a broken tail.

How could a man like that be involved in anything illegal? He couldn't be. She simply couldn't be that wrong about him.

She dipped her fingers into the milk and repeated the process of getting them into the calf's mouth. "If he's blind, he'll learn to cope. No one is perfect. We all have to learn to deal with our flaws."

When he didn't say anything, Mandy looked up. She didn't understand the yearning she saw in his eyes. "What kind of flaws do you have?" he asked at last.

"Too many to enumerate."

"I don't believe that. Name one."

Her pulse stirred at the intensity of his gaze sending flutters all through her body.

"I wear size ten shoes." Making a joke seemed easier than revealing too much about herself.

"That's not exactly a flaw." The light in

his eyes changed. He withdrew and the loss was as sharp as a thorn under her skin.

"I'll never be as good a cop as my father," she admitted in a rush.

Garrett tipped his head slightly to study her. "Why is that important?"

"Because I loved him. I wanted him to be proud of me. He was killed in a drug raid. The men who worked with him said he was incredibly brave. I want to be like him, but I'm not."

"I think you are. My father is the last man on earth I want to be like."

"Why?" She really wanted to know.

"Ina would have called him mean and ugly. He drank too much."

"I'm sorry."

"No big deal." He shrugged it off, but Mandy wasn't fooled. It was a big deal.

The calf began to suckle more eagerly on Mandy's hand. "I think he's getting the hang of it."

"Try the nipple again," Garrett suggested.

Mandy reassembled the feeder and tried once more to get the calf to suck by stroking his throat once she had the bottle in his mouth. He gave one firm pull.

"That's a good boy," she crooned.

He responded with a second and a third suck quickly followed by more.

Mandy grinned at Garrett. "He's doing it."

"I see that. You have the touch."

Delighted by his praise, she stroked the calf's head. "What are we going to call him?"

"He's not out of the woods yet. Maybe we should wait to name him."

She liked that he said "we." "I think we should call him Joey."

"Guess it's as good a name as any."

"I'm ashamed to admit, I live in the middle of cattle country, but I don't actually know much about them. Why isn't he out of the woods?"

"He needs to be able to stand or his lungs will fill with fluid and he'll die."

"Joey is *not* going to die."

"Because you say so?"

"Yes," she stated firmly.

Garrett looked skeptical. "And do you always get your way?"

Casting a glance at him from the corner of her eye, she shrugged. "Not always, but wearing a gun has improved my statistics."

He laughed. She loved the deep timbre of the sound.

Smiling at her, he said, "I didn't know cops had a sense of humor."

"Oh, yes. We can be a barrel of laughs. A gun barrel that is."

"Not the ones I've known," he replied.

She arched her brows. "And you've known a lot?"

His smile disappeared. He looked down at the calf. "A few more than I would have liked, but you knew that already, didn't you?"

"I knew you'd been arrested for possession of marijuana and meth and served two months."

"Yeah."

"In my career I've found that there is usually more to the story than the official report."

"So, if I told you it was Judy's stash and that I didn't know she'd hidden it under the seat of my truck, you'd believe me?"

"Is that what happened?"

Their little patient had finished with his meal and laid his head on Garrett's leg. Shifting Joey's weight to a more comfortable position, Garrett avoided looking at Mandy. "Does it matter?"

Mandy set the empty bottle aside and stroked Joey's head. "Would you believe me if I said that it didn't?"

Garrett eyes met hers. "I'm not sure."

Mandy drew her knees up and wrapped her arms around them. "Everyone makes mistakes. I've made mistakes. Big ones that have hurt innocent people. I have to live with that."

"Living with them — that's the hard part, isn't it?" he said quietly, staring toward the barn door and the house beyond.

His voice held such an odd quality that a shiver of foreboding skittered over Mandy's nerve endings.

She wanted to reassure him, to offer him comfort, but for what she wasn't sure. "Only God is perfect, Garrett. The rest of us are merely human."

When he didn't answer, she reached out and laid her hand over his where it rested on Joey's neck. Her touch jerked his attention back from wherever it had gone.

He glanced from her hand to her face. His pupils darkened as their eyes met. His gaze traveled over her features one by one until it came to rest on her mouth. Her lips tingled under his scrutiny.

He was going to kiss her.

TEN

Mandy's heart thudded against the inside of her chest and sent her pulse racing. A dozen disjointed thoughts tumbled through her mind. She barely knew him. She was crazy to be thinking about kissing him.

He reached out and drew his fingertips along the edge of her jaw with exquisite tenderness as he tucked a strand of her hair behind her ear. She didn't pull away.

The sudden sound of Ina's voice broke the tenuous thread between them. "I figured if you was gonna try and save the little runt this might help."

She carried a quilt in her arms, which she held out to them over the stall door.

Mandy rose to her feet hoping Ina didn't notice the flush on her face. Taking the blanket, Mandy was surprised by its heat.

"I tumbled it in the dryer to get it nice and warm," Ina admitted with a sheepish look.

Mandy took back every harsh thought she'd had about Ina's attitude. The old gal had a soft heart beneath her tough exterior after all.

Carrying the quilt to Garrett, Mandy helped him wrap it around Joey until only the calf's head stuck out.

Ina folded her arms on the top of the gate. "If you can get him strong enough to stand, you might be able to get one of the other nursing cows to adopt him."

Mandy brightened. "Will they do that?"

"Sometimes," Garrett replied slowly.

"It's worth a try," Mandy insisted.

Ina straightened. "I'll go put another quilt in the dryer and we can trade them out when they get cool."

Throughout the night they took turns working to keep Joey warm, coaxing him to eat and trying to help him stand. While Mandy and Garrett worked with the calf, Ina kept watch over Colin and brought out a rewarmed quilt when they needed one.

Sometime around four o'clock in the morning, Ina came out to take a turn in the barn and sent Mandy to the house.

Grateful for the break, Mandy checked to see that Colin was sleeping quietly, then she settled herself on the sofa and leaned her head back for a few minutes.

210

The next thing she knew, Wiley was pawing at her leg. Prying her eyes open, Mandy glanced out the windows. The eastern sky glowed faintly with hues of rose and gold, but the sun wasn't up.

Wiley whined and trotted over to sit in front of the crib. Looking that way, Mandy saw Colin peeking at her between the crib rails.

She sat up and smiled at him. "Hey, little man. Remember me?"

He gurgled happily, slobbering on his fist as he tried to get the whole thing in his mouth.

"Wait right there. I'll get your bottle." She headed into the kitchen, happy to find Garrett had several bottles lined up in the refrigerator.

It took her only a few minutes to warm the formula and change Colin's diaper. Lifting him out of his crib, she settled into the recliner with him, taking care not to jar his injured shoulder.

Wiley took her vacated spot on the sofa and laid his head on his paws, but he never took his eyes off Colin.

Unlike Joey, Colin had no hesitation about downing his food. When he was finished, Mandy snuggled him upright beneath her chin. Warm and content, he gave a sailor-like belch and soon drifted off to sleep. Mandy leaned back a little more in the chair.

This child — Garrett's child — fit perfectly in her arms. Without trying, Colin had filled a place in her heart she hadn't known was empty. Laying her cheek on his head, she breathed in the milky, baby scent of him and relished the warm feel of him next to her skin.

Time went by and the light grew in the east, but Mandy couldn't bring herself to lay him down in his crib.

Garrett walked into his house with the intention of giving Mandy the news that Joey had managed to stand on his own wobbly legs and take his first steps. What he saw when he glanced in the living room stopped him in his tracks.

Mandy had fallen asleep in his chair. Colin lay curled on her chest.

With their same shade of blond hair and the sweet smiles on their faces, they could easily have been mistaken for mother and son. The vision caused unshed tears to sting Garrett's eyes.

Judy would have held Colin like that, her arm curved around him, holding him safe even in sleep. Why had someone taken her life? The thought that he might never know left him empty, sad and angry.

Memories of his marriage were bittersweet. He'd wanted so badly to love Judy and to be loved in return.

It seemed his whole life had been made up of wanting something he couldn't have. Wanting his father to stop hitting him, wanting his mother to come home, wanting Judy to care enough to stay. Now, he wanted something even more unobtainable.

He wanted the woman holding his son.

He might as well covet the moon. Mandy worried that she wasn't as brave as her father. She'd never respect a man who didn't possess the kind of courage she admired.

Garrett leaned his shoulder against the archway and watched them sleeping. A smile curved his lips. Simple pleasures were rare in his life, but this was one he would call out of his memory for years to come, the sight of Mandy holding his son.

Caring so much for her was a mistake. He wouldn't give another woman the chance to walk away from him.

Even as the thought formed, he realized he was fighting a losing battle against his growing affection for Mandy.

The need to send her away before his

heart was torn apart wasn't half as strong as the need to cherish her and keep her near.

As he watched silently, longing for things that could never be, her eyes fluttered open. She blinked, then squinted at him. "What time is it?"

"Seven."

Sitting up carefully, she shifted Colin's weight to the crook of her arm. "How's Joey?"

"Standing."

"He is?" Joy brightened her face.

Garrett straightened. "A few wobbly minutes was all he managed, but it's a start."

"That's great. You must be exhausted." She scooted forward in the chair and tried to rise, but winced in pain. Wiley looked on from the sofa.

Crossing the room, Garrett lifted Colin from her. "I might be in bad shape, but I think you're in worse shape."

"You really know how to flatter a woman."

"Sorry."

He didn't know much about women and he certainly didn't know how to behave with one who was the sheriff. He turned away and laid Colin in the crib without waking him.

Rising, Mandy stretched and rolled her shoulders. "Where's Ina?"

His hands itched to cup Mandy's shoulders and knead her pain away, but he knew if he touched her, he'd have to kiss her. He pushed his hands deep in his pockets. "She went home about an hour ago."

"I should get going, too. I have to be at the office by nine and I really need a shower."

He sniffed loudly. "No comment."

"You're no petunia yourself, buddy." A scowl put a furrow between her brows, but there was a twinkle in her eyes.

"Guilty as charged."

"What time should I come back?"

"Back?"

"Won't Joey need to be fed and cared for around the clock? Between him and Colin, you can't do it all."

She was offering to lend a hand. A quiet happiness settled in Garrett's chest. "Aren't you forgetting that you have a job?"

"I multitask and I delegate well. Besides, my mother is always telling me that I need a hobby. Helping raise Joey will be an excellent project, although I imagine Mom was thinking more along the lines of knitting or tennis."

"Are you sure Joey isn't an excuse to keep an eye on Colin?" He knew he sounded defensive, but he couldn't help it.

Raking her hair back with both hands, she gathered it at the nape of her neck and held it a second before letting it spill loose again. "Okay, guilty as charged, too. I adore your son. I'd love to see more of him. If that's okay with you."

Don't do it. Don't let her into your life. She won't stay. No one ever does.

Clenching his teeth until they ached, he hardened his heart against the yearning to have her near.

Her eyes filled with soft pleading as she took a step closer. "Please?"

Did she have any idea how beautiful she looked in the morning light? How could he deny her? The truth was, he didn't want to. He gave in, knowing he'd regret his decision, but at this moment, the pain seemed worth the risk.

"If you come back this evening, I'll let you take over for a few hours while I grab a nap."

"Great. I'll be back right after supper."

Wiley exploded off the sofa, barking wildly and leaping in circles. Startled, Mandy jumped backward and collided with Garrett. He grabbed her arms to steady her. Colin began crying.

Their quiet interlude came to a noisy end. Mandy laughed. "I can't believe you taught the dog to do that."

Her bright smile drew one from Garrett. He reluctantly dropped his hands from her shoulders and picked up his squalling son. "It was funnier before there was a baby to wake up."

"As I was saying, I'll come out after s-u-p-p-e-r."

She was coming back. The thought drove the shadows of Garrett's past into retreat. Maybe, just maybe, Sheriff Amanda Scott was the one person who could keep them at bay.

She said, "If you want, I can even take Colin with me to church Sunday morning. You can get some rest while we're gone."

"You really are determined to get him into church, aren't you?"

"I believe it's important."

"Even at his age?"

"I consider it important at any age to be a part of God's family."

To be part of a family. What would that be like? "I'll think about it."

Stepping closer, Mandy reached out to stroke Colin's hair. "You're welcome to come, too."

"Me? To church?"

"If you've never tried it, how do you know you won't like it? Give God a chance. Knowing His love changes everything."

Garrett shook his head. "God had His shot with me and He blew it."

"I'm sorry you feel that way. I'm sorry something happened that made you turn your back on God, but He's waiting for you to find Him again. Faith grows from the tiniest of seeds. Maybe Colin is that seed in your life."

Or maybe Mandy was. "If you're as persistent at tracking down criminals as you are in arguing for God, then Timber Wells is gonna be crime-free in no time."

She sent a beaming smile his way. "Does that mean you'll come?"

"That means I'll think about it."

After spending an unusually quiet Saturday afternoon in her office, Mandy stopped to pick up a fast food supper, then headed home to change into boots, jeans and a comfortable cotton shirt. Wolfing down the last bite of her burger, she pulled a bottle of water from the fridge and headed toward the door. Before she reached it, her cell phone rang.

A rush of frustration hit her. She could only hope it wasn't something that would keep her from returning to the ranch. The realization of just how much she wanted to see Garrett and Colin amazed her.

Snapping open the phone, she relaxed when she saw it was her mother.

"Mandy, I hope you aren't busy." Kathryn's cheerful voice sounded just a shade too cheerful.

"Actually, I am."

"Oh. I thought maybe you'd be free this evening. I just ran into Candice and we were hoping you could join us for dinner."

Mandy wasn't fooled. "You were hoping I could join you, Candice, and Candice's unmarried doctor son for dinner."

There was a long pause. Then her mother said, "It was just a thought. I didn't want you spending the evening alone."

"Thanks for thinking of me, but I've got plans."

"You do?"

"Don't sound so shocked, Mom."

"I'm not shocked. I'm just disappointed that you can't join us. I guess I'll see you at church tomorrow."

"Of course."

Mandy ended the call and slipped the phone in the pocket of her jeans. She couldn't really be mad. Her mom's heart was in the right place.

How would her mother feel if she knew Mandy had turned down dinner with an eligible doctor to spend an evening with

Garrett?

Mandy blew out a long breath. She wasn't quite ready to have that conversation.

There was plenty of daylight left by the time Mandy finally reached the ranch. The days were growing longer as spring progressed into summer. In Garrett's pasture, his herd of cattle contentedly munched grass as their offspring frolicked around them. It was an endearing sight.

Garrett came out of the house to greet her as she pulled in. His tentative smile made her wonder if he thought the closeness they'd shared the previous night might have vanished in the light of day.

For her part, it hadn't, but she couldn't be sure what he was thinking.

"Your relief has arrived," she said hoping to coax a smile from him. It worked.

"Just in the knick of time. I was about to fall asleep on my feet."

"How's Joey doing?"

"Better than I expected."

"Any luck getting another cow to adopt him?"

Garrett shook his head. "Not yet, but I haven't given up. I had the vet out to see him today. He confirmed that Joey's almost completely blind and that he'll be a dwarf. He's not sure how long the little fellow will survive, but he's doing okay for now."

It wasn't the best news, but that didn't mean she was going to give up trying to save him. "What do you need me to do?"

"If you could watch Colin and feed Joey while I grab a few hours of sleep that'd be great."

"I think I can manage that."

A slow grin spread across his face. "I think you can manage just about anything you set your mind to."

"Compliments will get you a long way in my book. Where is my human charge for the evening?"

Garrett nodded toward the door. "He's already in his stroller, which has come in very handy since you talked me into buying the thing."

"There you go. It pays to trust my judgment." Mandy followed Garrett into the house and collected Colin.

A few hours later, she was seated on a bale of hay inside Joey's stall, laughing at the calf's wobbly attempts to frisk around the enclosure. He held his head turned slightly to one side, which made Mandy suspect he could see a little on that side. While he might thump into the wooden sides of the stall occasionally, his ability to find the bottle in Mandy's hand was unerring.

Colin and his canine guardian, Wiley, were parked just outside Joey's pen. Colin, leaning back in his stroller, was intent on grasping Wiley's wagging tail, but wasn't having much success. His happy giggle as the fringe of Wiley's crooked tail swept over his palm made Mandy smile, too.

Her feelings toward Colin were straightforward and maternal. Her feelings toward his father were anything but simple. She wasn't sure how she felt about her relationship with Garrett, or where she wanted it to go.

If it was a relationship.

Wiley suddenly darted toward the entrance, and Mandy saw Garrett walking toward her. The burst of happiness that swept through her made her smile as he approached.

Her head might tell her to be careful, that Garrett wouldn't easily share his life, but her heart was telling her that this man had become very special to her. There was a reason God had brought them together.

Colin, bereft of his playmate, began to fuss.

"Hey, little man, what's the problem?" Garrett stooped to pick up his son.

Instantly quieted by the sound of Garrett's voice. Colin grinned and patted his father's face. The love Mandy saw shinning in Garrett's eyes melted her heart. The last faint reserve in the back of her mind vanished.

Father and son belonged together. They were going to do just fine.

Garrett felt Mandy's gaze on him. When he looked her way, he saw the soft sparkle of tears in her eyes. He frowned in concern. "Are you okay?"

She sniffed and rubbed her hands over her face. "I'm fine."

Opening the gate, he walked in and took a seat beside her on the hay bale. Colin immediately reached for her and Garrett allowed her to take the child. "He likes you."

Sniffing once more, she said, "The feeling is completely mutual."

Joey, attracted by another arrival in his pen, came over to investigate. Not finding another bottle, he folded his legs and dropped into a heap in front of them and laid his head on Garrett's boot.

"You seem to have a way with babies, too," Mandy observed.

"Are you trying to say I'm a soft touch?"

She laid a hand over his. "A sickly calf, a meal-obsessed dog, a motherless baby — call me crazy, but yes, I think you're a dyedin-the-wool softy, Garrett."

The sound of his name on her lips, the touch of her hand sent warmth spiraling through him. He couldn't remember ever feeling so alive, so full of hope. Mandy had given him that.

Was she the key that could lock his painful past out of his mind for good? He wanted that to be true as much as he'd ever wanted anything.

"If I'm a soft touch, you're just as bad. Look who's spoiling the baby?"

She ran her fingers through Colin's curls. "Maybe I'm trying to make up for the fact that I haven't been able to discover who killed his mother. It's so sad that he'll never know her."

"Kids survive." Garrett tried to keep the bitterness out of his voice.

"At least you'll be able to fill in some of the blanks for him when he's older."

"If he asks."

She looked at him sharply. "Of course he'll ask. Why wouldn't he? You must have asked your father questions about your mother."

Garrett tensed. "What do you know about that?"

"Just that your mother left when you were small. I didn't mean to upset you."

His head began pounding. "I'm not upset. I didn't need to ask about her. She was gone and that was that."

Rising to his feet, he lifted Colin out of her arms. "I should get him to bed."

"Okay." Her puzzled tone told him he'd overreacted.

He tried to repair the damage. "I'm sorry, I'm just tired. I guess the nap wasn't enough to take the edge off."

"How are you going to manage tonight?"

"Joey's doing well enough that I won't have to spend the night with him. I'll just get up for a couple of feedings. If worse comes to worst, I can make a place for him in the house."

She stood. "Well, if you have it figured out, I should probably get going."

They left the stall and began walking toward the front of the barn. Colin had fallen asleep in Garrett's arms. At Mandy's truck, they both paused by unspoken consent. Twilight had fallen and the stars were beginning to appear.

He didn't want her to leave. Having her near made everything seem possible. "Thanks for helping out today, Mandy. I mean that."

"I was glad to do it. I'll see you after work tomorrow."

"You don't have to do that."

"I want to. Besides, raising Joey is my hobby, remember?"

He didn't care what excuse she used. He just wanted her to come back.

As Mandy drove away, he couldn't help but remember standing in the same spot, waiting for his mother to come home. Years later, it had been Judy he waited for. They had never returned.

Would it really be different this time?

Eleven

Mandy slammed down the phone in frustration. "If they won't talk to me without a subpoena, I'll get them one."

As much as it irked her to admit it, she knew she didn't have enough evidence for one at this point.

"Who was that?" Donna asked from the doorway where she stood with a stack of papers in her hands.

"That was the uncooperative corporate office of Global Shipping."

Advancing into the room, Donna pulled open a filing cabinet and began inserting pages into folders. "Are you missing an order, too? They lost my red beaded evening bag with rhinestone clasp. Global claims it was never shipped, but the Shopping Warehouse insists it was. I bet I'll never get my money back."

"I didn't call them about an order." Mandy hesitated, then said, "I've got a hunch I wanted to follow up on, but the company won't give me any information without a subpoena."

Donna turned around. "What kind of hunch?"

"The company has been making a lot of deliveries to your apartment complex. I want to make sure they're all legitimate."

Donna's eyebrows shot up. "You think there's something fishy going on in my complex? Is it Mr. Dobbs? I've seen him getting a lot of packages. Do you think it's pornography? I could start keeping the place under surveillance for you."

Mandy almost chuckled at the eagerness in Donna's voice, but managed to stop herself. Donna might actually be able to help. "It wouldn't hurt to keep an eye out, note any suspicious goings-on."

"I'll start a log. What should I do if see something?"

"Nothing. Just let me know."

Mandy picked up the phone and began dialing Tom Wick's number. "I'm going to see what the county attorney thinks my chances of getting a subpoena are."

Donna closed the file drawer. "You're like a dog with a bone when you get an idea, Sheriff."

"I'll take that as a compliment, Donna."

If determination could get her answers, Mandy had more than enough to spare.

"Where are you off to tonight?" Kathryn asked.

Mandy paused in the process of closing her front door. Her mother was seated on the nearby porch swing with her Bible in her lap.

"I'm going to check on Colin Bowen."

"Seems to me you've been checking on that boy a lot."

"I guess I have been."

"Are you still worried his father isn't taking care of him properly?"

"No, it's not that. Garrett is doing a great job."

"Then why all the visits?"

Sighing deeply, Mandy crossed the gray painted boards and sat down next to her mother. The scent of sage and roses from the flower beds bordering the walk tinted the warm afternoon air. Not much moved it in the summer heat except for a few bees flitting from flower to flower.

The creak of the swing chains filled the silence until Kathryn said, "I didn't mean to pry."

"I know that."

"If you have something you'd like to talk

about, I'm listening."

"I'm not sure if it is something I want to talk about yet."

"Then you're about the only person in Timber Wells who isn't discussing it."

Mandy turned to look at her mother in surprise. "What?"

"Did you think it would go unnoticed that our sheriff, a single woman, is seeing a single man on a regular basis?"

"I guess I thought the people of this town had better things to talk about."

"The price of wheat, the price of cattle, the price of gas and gossip. That's what gets talked about in this town."

"There's nothing scandalous going on between Garrett and me."

"I didn't think for a moment that there was."

"Then why are we having this conversation?"

Kathryn laid a hand on Mandy's arm. "You sat down beside me."

Her mother was right. Mandy did need to talk. "I like him, Mom. I like him a lot, but I can't get over the feeling that he's keeping something from me."

"Something to do with his ex-wife's death?"

"I don't think so. I think it's deeper than that."

"Okay, now you're scaring me."

"Sorry. I see so many good things in Garrett, but I don't think he sees them in himself. He never talks about his childhood or about his parents. I know he must have been deeply affected by his mother's desertion, but he claims he wasn't."

"How is he handling fatherhood?"

Mandy smiled. "He's so gentle with Colin. He never gets upset or loses his temper."

"Which one are you more attracted to? The father or the child?"

"It would be easier to say the baby, but that wouldn't be the truth. I care for both of them. Very much."

"That wasn't so hard to admit, was it?"

Mandy grinned. "No, it wasn't hard to admit. I just wish Garrett shared our faith."

"He's not a Christian?"

"No, but I see a longing for God on his face when I talk about church and what it means to me. It's almost as if he is afraid to trust God."

Garrett's lack of faith was the one thing that kept Mandy from allowing herself to imagine a future with him.

"Honey, if there is anyone whose light can shine the way for him, it's you. I'm going to pray for you both." She opened her Bible again.

Rising, Mandy planted a kiss on her mother's head. "Thanks. There's no one I'd rather have put in a good word for me."

"Will you be at Bible study class Monday?"

"I'm planning on it."

"Why don't you invite Mr. Bowen? I'd like to meet him and his son."

"I don't think he'll come, Mom."

"Invite him anyway," Kathryn said. "We might both be surprised. God nudges people in the right direction by many different ways."

On Sunday morning, Mandy was seated in her usual spot in the last pew of the Prairie View Community Church. Knowing she might be called out at any time, she always sat closest to the back. That way, she wouldn't have to disturb the rest of the congregation if she had to leave during the service.

At the moment, her thoughts weren't on the song the choir was singing so beautifully. It was her caseload of unsolved crimes that weighed on her mind. She'd been unable to get a subpoena for the shipping company records, but that didn't mean she'd given up. With Donna's help, she hoped to uncover a pattern of unusual activity that would be enough to convince a judge that her request was justified.

She had nothing new in Judy's murder. To make matters worse, both J. J. and the truckers who'd sideswiped Mandy's SUV were out of jail on bail.

She had extended her mother's invitation to Garrett, but he hadn't accepted. The best she got was his usual, "I'll think about it."

The organ music swelled as the service was about to begin. Mandy reached for her hymnal to join in. The sound of the outside door opening made her glance over her shoulder. To her complete amazement, Garrett walked in with Colin in his infant seat.

Garrett's worried expression lightened as he recognized her. He nodded slightly. She took a step over, sending an unspoken invitation to join her.

He slipped into the pew beside her and set Colin on the seat between them. The baby was dressed in the red plaid vest with the little red bow tie she'd purchased for him at the yard sale. Mandy leaned toward Garrett and whispered. "I knew he'd look cute in it."

Still seeming ill at ease, Garrett nodded

and pulled at the collar of his own blue dress shirt. "Let's hope he stays cute and asleep."

"There's a cry room if you need it. Or you could take him to the nursery."

"That's good to know," Garrett whispered back.

She handed him the song book. "I'm glad you're here."

"It's all your fault."

Their conversation, quiet as it was, drew a few scowls and curious looks from the people seated in front of them. Mandy smiled brightly and nodded in return. Nothing could temper the joy singing through her soul. Garrett had come to church.

She prayed that he would one day come to know Jesus as his Lord and Savior.

Garrett tried to keep his focus on the sermon, but it was hard with Mandy sitting so close. Her insistence that he should honor Judy's desire to have Colin raised in a Christian home had brought him here today. While he wasn't sure he needed God, he was willing to explore the faith both Judy and Mandy held in such high regard.

When the service was over, he followed Mandy outside. Some of the churchgoers left quickly, but many others had divided up into groups of family and friends and were visiting in the shade of the pear trees that lined the street in front of the church.

The sight was a pointed reminder that he wasn't welcome in their circles. He had no family and very few friends.

Mandy waved to someone and then grabbed Garrett's arm, preventing him from leaving. A woman in her early fifties and wearing a pale blue suit approached them with a speculative light in her eyes. Eyes the same shape and color as Mandy's.

"Mom, I'd like you to meet Garrett Bowen. Garrett, this is my mother, Kathryn Scott."

Garrett's heart jumped into his throat and seemed prepared to stay lodged there. "Ma'am."

"Mr. Bowen, I've been hearing good things about you from my daughter. This must be Colin. Oh, he is cute." She leaned toward his son, now awake in his carrier.

Garrett glanced at Mandy. So she had been telling her mother good things about him. He liked the sound of that.

Would that all change once Mandy found out about his past? He wanted to believe it wouldn't. He wanted to believe she would understand, but it was hard to. He was so used to being alone, relying on no one but himself.

A second woman approached. Garrett recognized her as the dispatcher who worked at the courthouse. "Mr. Bowen, it's nice to see you worshiping with us this morning."

"Thanks."

Donna turned to Mandy. "I noticed Fred wasn't in church this morning. Do you have him pulling some overtime?"

Mandy, too, had noticed his absence from the choir. "He's not working. It's Ken's turn to cover this weekend."

Donna folded her arms. "That's odd."

Kathryn Scott gave up tickling Colin's chubby cheeks and said, "Mr. Bowen, I was very sorry to hear about your wife's death."

"Ex-wife, but thank you."

"I'm sure my daughter will discover who is responsible. She's very tenacious."

"Unfortunately, I don't have much to go on at this point," Mandy admitted.

"The case has gone cold," Donna added with a sad shake of her head. "We may never find out what happened."

Garrett caught the faint frown Mandy leveled at Donna. "That's why I've decided to ask for the public's help. I'm running a piece in several area newspapers asking for any information. I've included a photo of

236

Judy and a description of her car. I'm hoping someone saw her that morning and will come forward."

"When did you decide this?" Donna asked.

"This morning."

Looking over Mandy's head, Garrett saw Ina Purdy walking toward him. She had traded in her jeans and oversized work shirt for a navy pant suit. "I was just fixing to call you, Garrett. I'm surprised to see you here."

"I'm a little surprised myself."

"Guess our sheriff is having a good influence on you. Are you still planning on going to that Colorado sale?"

"If you're still planning on keeping Colin for me."

The summer sale on the Conway ranch was the biggest sale in southern Colorado. Buyers from all over the country would be there. Besides his contracts with six Kansas ranchers to be filled, Garrett was going to buy cows for his own herd.

To produce the high-quality cattle he wanted to breed, he needed high-quality cows and the Conway ranch produced some of the finest Angus cattle in the business.

Garrett was building his son's legacy. He intended to do it right.

Ina waved one hand. " 'Course I'll watch

him. I've decided to let you pick up a new bull for me. That is, if the price is right."

He rubbed his chin. "A Conway bull isn't gonna be cheap."

"I know, but I trust you to find me a bargain."

A measure of pride filled Garrett at her faith in him. "We can discuss your price range before I take off tomorrow."

"You're leaving town?" Mandy asked, a faint look of concern on her face.

"Just for a couple of days." Would she miss him? He was sure going to miss her.

"Who's going to take care of Joey?" she asked softly.

Ina rolled her eyes. "That would be me. 'Course, you're welcome to come lend a hand. A body my age shouldn't be working day and night. It's likely to drive me to an early grave. At least I don't have to keep that dog."

Spinning around, she headed toward her truck parked at the curb.

Kathryn's attention was claimed by another group of women. She excused herself and she and Donna left. Garrett found himself alone with Mandy.

She glanced around, then smiled at him warmly. "I'm glad you came today."

"Are you?"

"Of course I am. The real question would be, are you glad you came?"

"I am. It felt nice."

"That's a start."

Garrett wanted to believe that it was. If God had seen fit to bring Mandy and Colin into his life, then maybe He had been listening all those years ago.

Mandy breathed a sigh of relief the next afternoon when she saw Garrett's truck and trailer still parked at the ranch. He hadn't left yet.

He might only be leaving for a few days, but she was missing him already.

He opened the door before she knocked. Had he been watching for her? There was a soft light in his eyes that made her believe he had been. Wiley jumped around her feet, apparently happy to see her, too.

"I was afraid I'd missed you. I got tied up at work." Mandy noticed Ina standing in the living room and nodded in her direction. "Mrs. Purdy. Nice to see you."

Ina fisted her hands on her hips. "Is someone from your office gonna do something about those kids? I had to call again last night."

Taken aback, Mandy said, "I'm sorry, but this is the first I've heard of it. What's the

239

problem?"

"Those high school hooligans have been holding their keg parties in the old barn across the section from my place. All that loud music and carrying on. I ran them off last month. I told them I'd sic the sheriff on them if they came back. Last night, I saw them out there again."

"I'll certainly check it out."

"Hmm! That's what your deputy said, but I don't expect he did anything and I know why."

"Which deputy was that?"

Ina folded her arms over her bony chest. "Ken Holt. I told him what I saw. I'm not surprised he didn't tell you."

"Why do you say that?"

" 'Cause his little brother was the one with the keg in the back of his pickup. Luke Holt's a wild one. That boy's looking for serious trouble."

Was Ken's brother the "personal problem" Ken had been having? If he'd been covering up Luke's illegal activities, Ken was in some serious trouble himself.

"You say they were there again last night and you reported it?" Ken had been on duty.

"I did. Someone's gonna get hurt in that old place if you don't put a stop to it."

"I'll speak to Ken tomorrow." Mandy

would listen to his side of the story, but Ina's account raised some troubling issues.

Slightly mollified, Ina lifted Colin's infant seat and slipped a large diaper bag over her shoulder. "Guess I should get going so you can get on the road, Garrett. Remember, I need a proven bull, not one of their untried yearlings."

"I remember." He and Mandy exchanged amused glances as they followed Ina out the door.

Garrett helped secure Colin's car seat in Ina's truck. When he was done, he pulled a piece of paper from his pocket and held it out. "This is Colin's schedule. He normally sleeps until six. After that, he gets his first bottle and some rice cereal."

Ina grabbed the list out of Garrett's hands. "Oh, for pity's sake. I managed to raise three kids of my own. I think I can watch your boy for a few days."

"I'm sure you can. It's just that I haven't left him for so long."

"And you haven't left him yet. Are you going? Or are you gonna dither here until the sale is over?"

"I'm going."

"Well, kiss the gal and then get on the road."

Mandy felt herself blushing even as a rush

of red crept up Garrett's neck.

Ina, with a merry cackle, started her truck and drove off.

As the dust settled, Garrett turned to Mandy. Reaching out, he gently cupped her cheek. "Guess I should follow orders."

"I think she was kidding."

"I'm not." Bending his head, he kissed her with great tenderness. Mandy's heart turned over with sweet joy as his lips moved over hers. This was so right.

After a long, wonderful moment, he pulled away. Cupping her cheek, he said, "I never thought I'd feel this way about anyone. I wish I didn't have to leave. There is so much I want to tell you."

Mandy smiled at him. "I'll be here when you get back, Garrett. I'm not going anywhere."

The following morning, Mandy tucked the memory of Garrett's kiss inside her heart and put on her professional face. She couldn't put off this interview any longer. Pressing the intercom button, she said, "Donna, have Ken step into my office, please."

Bleary-eyed and exhausted-looking, Ken entered the room and stood in front of her desk without meeting her gaze.

Repeating the story as Ina had relayed it, Mandy waited for Ken to deny the accusations or offer an explanation. He did neither. Instead, he said, "You'll have my resignation on your desk today."

"Ken, that wasn't what I wanted to hear. If you're having family problems, I can understand that. If you need time off, I can arrange it."

"Luke has been living with me since our folks split up. He's troubled, he's acting out, but he's a good kid. Ask Donna. She's spent time with him. Yeah, he gets detention sometimes, but he's just going through a rough patch."

"Ken, you know I want to help, but falsifying a crime report is serious. You aren't helping Luke by letting things like underage drinking slide by."

"I can't arrest my baby brother. I think it's best that I resign."

"I won't accept it. I'm ordering you to take a thirty-day leave of absence. If, at that time, you still feel you can't do this job, then I'll accept your resignation. I'm also going to suggest that you and your brother get some professional family counseling." The department would be shorthanded but Mandy knew the other officers would pick up the slack to help her.

Ken nodded. "I'll think about it."

After he left, Mandy opened the crime scene report that had arrived with the morning mail. The lab techs had been able to pull a partial print from one of the bags of meth that had been seized from the cattle truck.

The print was a match to an unknown set that had been lifted at her farm supply robbery. It was further proof that the meth had been manufactured nearby.

A knock at the door made her look up as Donna peeked in. "There is a Jessica Nichols who wants to see you."

The name rang a bell, but Mandy couldn't place a face with it. "Did she say what she wanted?"

"No, just that she needed to talk to you."

"Okay, send her in."

Mandy smiled politely as a middle-aged woman with salt-and-pepper hair came forward with a timid air. She was wearing a blue-and-white waitress uniform.

As soon as Mandy saw the outfit, the name clicked. Jessica waited tables at the all-night diner just down the street.

"Miss Nichols, what can I do for you?" Mandy indicated the chair opposite her desk.

Jessica slipped into it. Smoothing the front

of her skirt to erase the wrinkle, she clasped her hands together. "I wasn't going to come because I don't know how important this might be, but my boss said I should. I saw the woman in the paper."

"What woman?"

"The one who was killed in that car accident."

Mandy leaned forward. "You saw Judy Bowen?"

"I never knew her name until I read it in the paper, but I'm certain that's who I saw. She used to come into the diner late at night when she lived here about a year ago. She never left a tip."

"When was the last time you saw her?"

"The morning she died. I was walking home. I'd just gotten off my shift and I saw her pull up to the gas pump at Turner's Truck Stop."

"What time was this?"

"It was just before seven that morning."

The wreck had occurred less than ten minutes later. Mandy began taking notes. "You saw her getting gas."

Jessica leaned forward. "That's just it. She didn't get any."

Mandy stopped writing. "I'm not following you."

"She stopped at the pump and started to

walk into the store. But at the front door, she suddenly turned around and ran back to her car and drove off. I thought she must have forgotten her purse. I've done that myself."

"Did you see anyone follow her?"

"No. I turned the corner and didn't look back. I wish I had."

"Did you happen to notice which direction she came from?"

Jessica pressed one finger to her lips and tapped gently. "I think she came from the south. Yes, I'm sure of it because that's what made me think she must have forgotten something. She went back the way she'd come."

Judy had driven in from the south, not from the direction of Garrett's ranch which lay ten miles north of town. He'd been telling the truth. He hadn't seen Judy that day. Mandy had been right to believe in him. "Miss Nichols, did you notice any other vehicles parked in the area?"

"Just one of those blue-and-white delivery vans. Oh, and there was a tow truck there."

Had J. J. or Spike progressed from small-time crime to murder? Was that the reason J. J. had been so quick to pull a knife? Mandy had dismissed him as a junkie with bad judgment. Maybe she was underestimating him.

Frowning, Mandy asked, "Did you see the drivers?"

Shaking her head sadly, Jessica looked down and smoothed the front of her skirt again. "No. I'm sorry."

"When Judy used to come to your diner, did she come in alone?"

Jessica rolled her eyes at that. "She used to hang out with that weasel Spike Carver. I think they were doing drugs or something. I see a lot of messed-up people coming in at three o'clock in the morning. Most honest people are in bed by then — unless they have a job like mine. Have I been any help?"

"More than you know, Miss Nichols. Thank you for coming forward."

After the woman left, Mandy sat back in her chair and pondered what to make of this new information. Something or someone at Turner's Truck Stop had frightened Judy Bowen into bolting out of town. Less than ten minutes later, her car had been forced through a guardrail and she was dead.

Mandy rose and walked out into the common area. She saw Fred and Benny talking quietly at their desks. Ken had already left.

She said, "Benny, I want you to bring Spike Carver in for questioning. Fred, I want you to pick up J. J. again."

"Why?" Fred rose and pulled his gun from the drawer of his desk.

"Judy was at Turner's Truck Stop the morning she was killed."

Turning to Donna, Mandy said, "Give Aaron Turner and Mike Peters a call and ask them to come in, too."

Donna's face registered surprise. "You think they're involved?"

"Spike was a known associate of Judy before she left town last year. I have a lot of questions about him. Oh, and get me a DMV report on both J. J. and Spike. I want to know what kind of vehicles they drive."

Benny and Fred took off and Donna made the call while Mandy paced in front of the dispatcher's desk. When Donna hung up, she said, "They're on their way."

Twenty minutes later, Aaron and Mike walked in. Mandy wasn't sure which she disliked most. Mike's belligerent attitude or Aaron's overly friendly one. She interviewed them separately, but both men told the same story. Neither of them remembered seeing Judy Bowen, but both of them remembered that J. J. and Spike had been hanging out at the truck stop the morning she died.

It wasn't much help, but it was something. However, when Donna handed over the motor-vehicle reports, Mandy's hopes rose sharply. When Benny came in with Spike an hour later, Mandy was ready for him.

Inside the interview room painted a dull gray, Mandy sat in a wooden chair across a small table from Spike. He sat leaning back in his chair, trying to look relaxed. Mandy wasn't fooled.

Fred came in and stood behind Mandy. Leaning down, he whispered, "Looks like J. J. flew the coop. No one has seen him since he got out on bail."

That wasn't good news. Mandy turned her attention to Spike. "You used to do drugs with Judy Bowen."

He shrugged. "So?"

"So she's dead."

"I know."

Mandy opened the folder in front of her. "You drive a 1999 Ford pickup, don't you?"

"Yeah."

"What color is it?"

"Black. Why?"

"We have a witness who said Judy was run off the road by a black truck."

Spike sat up. "I didn't have anything to do with that."

Mandy folded her hands in front of her. "Did she owe you money? Was that why she bolted when she saw you?"

"I never saw her."

Fred stepped forward and pounded his fist on the table. "We're going to get a sample of paint from your truck and it's going to match the paint that transferred to Judy's car. You murdered her."

Spike licked his lips. "I wasn't driving my truck that morning. I loaned it to someone else."

Fred leaned closer. "Who?"

"I want a deal before I say anything else," Spike said quickly. He sat back and waited.

Mandy's gut told her something wasn't right. This was too easy.

Fred straightened and folded his arms. "Tell us what you know and we'll talk deal."

Spike's gaze darted between them. "Okay. Garrett Bowen was driving my truck that morning."

Mandy's mind screamed no, but she kept her composure with difficulty. "Why would you loan your truck to Mr. Bowen?"

"We're business partners. He pays me to cook meth. I deliver it to his place and he handles the distribution. That's all I'm gonna say until I talk to a lawyer."

Mandy left the interview room and turned to Fred who had followed her out. She raked her fingers through her hair. "I don't believe it. I've been out to Garrett's place a dozen times."

"He's got hundreds of acres he could hide a lab in. Just because he wasn't cooking it in his kitchen doesn't mean he's innocent. I knew he was guilty from the start. I'm going to get a search warrant."

Fred started down the hall, but stopped to look back. With a smirk, he said, "Bowen sure pulled the wool over your eyes."

Twelve

Garrett shifted Colin's carrier to his other hand and unlocked the front door. "Man, you're getting heavy. What's Ina been feeding you while I was gone, lead pellets?"

Colin kicked his feet and cooed. Wiley, wagging his tail frantically danced around the carrier and whined.

Smiling, Garrett pushed open his door. "Yeah, I missed him, too."

Garrett had been able to fill his orders and buy the cows for his own herd in record time. He'd left the sale a day early and had driven straight through because he needed to see his son. For the first time in his life, the idea of God as a loving father began to make sense.

Garrett was constantly amazed at the way his heart had expanded to encompass Colin and Mandy. He couldn't imagine his life without either one of them.

If only Mandy felt the same after he

confessed what a coward he'd been.

She wasn't expecting him back until tomorrow. Tomorrow he would tell her everything. If their relationship had any chance, there had to be honesty between them. Telling her would be hard, but he hoped, and prayed, that she would understand. His confidence wavered. What if she didn't understand? If he destroyed the evidence of his shame she never had to know any of it. He glanced over his head. That was what he needed to do.

Stepping into the living room, he set the carrier on the sofa and extracted Colin. Lifting the baby to settle him in his arms, Garrett was swamped with emotions deeper than he ever dreamed of. The feel of his son's small body, the sweet baby smell of his skin, the light in his bright eyes, wrapped a band around Garrett's heart and squeezed tight enough to bring tears of joy to his eyes.

"I love you, son. I'm never going to let a day go by without saying that."

Tenderly laying the baby in his crib, Garrett allowed his hand to linger on Colin's soft curls. "It's great to be home."

Home. A true home, the old house would become one at last.

Wiley's excited barking suddenly erupted from the kitchen. Leaving Colin happily batting at his moon and stars mobile, Garrett entered the kitchen, expecting Wiley to be sitting beside his dish demanding food, but instead the dog was at the front door.

When Garrett looked outside, he saw two squad cars parked in front of his house. Mandy, along with several of her deputies, stood on his porch.

Garrett opened the door. Mandy came forward and handed him a folded packet of papers. Her expression was cool and remote, but in her eyes he saw regret.

She said, "This is a warrant to search these premises."

"For what?" he demanded.

"It's all in the warrant."

She turned back to her men. "Fred, you and I will take the house and cellar. The rest of you take the barn and outbuildings."

Garrett had no idea what they were looking for, but with a sick, sinking sensation, he realized they would go upstairs.

Mandy didn't believe Garrett was trafficking in illegal drugs, but she knew he was hiding something. He was afraid of something. He sat quietly at the kitchen table, his copy of the search warrant in his hands, but his eyes darted to the doors at the back of the kitchen.

He'd seemed nervous when she was looking around the day Shari Compton made her home visit. At the time, Mandy had assumed Garrett was worried that Wiley's exuberance would spoil the social worker's report. Now, she wasn't so sure.

She said, "Fred, check the basement."

He nodded, opened the door and proceeded down the steps with caution. Garrett didn't so much as flinch, until she added, "I'll check upstairs."

His lips pressed into a tight white line and his eyes pleaded with her, but he didn't say a word.

The hinges squealed in protest as she pulled the door. Garrett made as if to rise, but Benny stopped him with a hand on his shoulder. "Wait right here, Mr. Bowen."

Mandy looked up the stairs. It was plain they hadn't been used in some time. A coat of dust covered everything except for a single set of boot prints and accompanying paw prints.

She looked over her shoulder. Garrett sat bent forward in the kitchen chair with his elbows resting on his knees. He wasn't watching her anymore. His face was turned away and resignation slumped his shoulders. What was he afraid of?

Walking up the steps, Mandy followed the path of the prints in the dust. They led first to the door on the right, but had made a circuit to each room and returned to this room before going back downstairs.

She opened the first room and stepped inside. Someone, she assumed it was Garrett, had walked to the closet. Looking down, she saw where the dog had sat beside Garrett. His tail had swept a small space clean.

She opened the door. It was empty except for some old clothing. That didn't make sense.

Pulling out her flashlight she made a careful check of the interior. Nothing.

She bit her lip as she pondered what he'd been doing staring into a nearly empty closet. She couldn't figure it out.

Rising on tiptoe, she patted along the shelf where she couldn't see. Suddenly, her fingers touched something metal. Pulling down the object, she saw it was an old-fashioned key.

A key to what?

Leaving the empty bedroom, she followed the footprints to the next room and again they stopped in front of the closet. When she tried to open it, she found it was locked.

She inserted the key. It turned over with a

grating click that made her flinch. Pulling open the door, Mandy stared into the empty space.

Two wire hangers on a dowel rod were the only evidence that the wardrobe had ever been used.

She stared into the narrow confines. Why keep an empty closet locked? This one didn't even have a shelf. Shining her light downward, she saw a dusty blue carpet square covering the floor. One corner was curled up slightly.

Leaning down she lifted the pad. The floor was covered with gouged out words, but the writing was upside-down.

Tipping her head, she read them and her blood ran cold.

Let me out. Make Dad stop hitting Mom. Help me, God. I hate him. Make him stop. Make him stop. Make him stop. G. B.

G. B. Garrett Bowen. Mandy stepped into the closet and sank to her knees. What had gone on here? Was this what Garrett wanted so badly to keep hidden?

Although the words had been scratched into the wood, Mandy knew it was his writing. Garrett had been locked in the closet.

She reached out and pulled the door closed. In the darkness, the only light was a thin band that shone from beneath the door, highlighting the words etched in that small rectangle of illumination.

Sympathy for Garrett gripped her heart until it ached with actual pain. Closing her eyes, she prayed for wisdom.

At least now she understood.

Rising to her feet, she pushed open the door and replaced the square of carpet covering his words. When Garrett was ready to talk about this, she would be there to listen.

After checking the rest of the rooms and finding nothing out of the ordinary, she replaced the key where she had found it and walked down the stairs. She closed the door to the stairwell and turned around to face Garrett.

She knew.

As soon as Garrett saw her face, he knew that she'd seen his writing on the floor.

Shame burned like acid in his throat. He dropped his head onto his hands and struggled not to be sick.

He should have torn those boards out years ago instead of leaving them locked away. As hard as he had tried, he'd never been able to lock away the memories or the anger or his shame.

Fred emerged from the basement, huffing

slightly. "I didn't find anything. You?"

Garrett felt Mandy's eyes on him, but he couldn't look at her. He steeled himself to face the humiliation of having his terrible secret exposed.

"There's nothing related to this case upstairs. Looks like our tip was wrong."

Garrett's gaze shot to meet hers. He was grateful for her silence, but he saw the pity he dreaded as much as his exposure.

Fred scowled. "Maybe he had time to move the stuff?"

Mandy said, "Either way, we're done in here. Go help Benny search the outbuildings."

When Fred was gone, Mandy sat at the table with Garrett. "I'm sorry. I hope you realize I'm just doing my job."

He turned his face away. "Sure, I get it. How can you trust a guy like me?"

"I do trust you, Garrett."

"You have a funny way of showing it."

"Why don't you tell me about the closet."

He stared down at his hands. "I was just a kid when I wrote that stuff. I don't know why I left it all these years."

"You must have been very scared."

Rubbing a hand along his jaw, he shot to his feet. He paced the length of the room and back. "My dad was a hard man, but when he drank, he got real mean. Mom and I never knew what would set him off."

"It wasn't your fault."

"I tried so hard to be invisible, but it didn't matter. If I so much as laid my fork down wrong at the dinner table, he'd start hitting me. When Mom tried to stop him, he'd drag me to the closet and lock me in, then he'd haul her to their bedroom and beat her senseless."

"And you heard it all."

"Every time. And every time I did nothing to help her."

"You were a child. There was nothing you could have done."

He whirled to face her and shouted, "I could have done something!"

"What happened to your mother, Garrett?"

The anger in his eyes faded. "I came home from school one day and she was gone. I can't really blame her for leaving him."

"She shouldn't have left you in that terrible situation."

"Why not? I left her in a worse situation every day of my life."

Turning away from Mandy, he said, "You should leave now."

He was shutting her out. She could feel his retreat and didn't know how to stop it.

"If you need someone to talk to —"

"I don't."

Mandy rose and laid a hand on his arm. He shrugged it off and stepped away. She had no choice but to leave, but her heart was breaking for him.

To Fred's disgust, the search of Garrett's outbuildings turned up nothing. He was in a sour mood as they drove back to town. Mandy didn't care. Spike had tried to implicate Garrett to save his own hide and it hadn't worked. Garrett was innocent.

When they walked into the station, Donna looked up expectantly. "I thought you were going to arrest Bowen? What happened?"

Mandy said, "Spike was lying."

"Maybe," Fred countered.

Shaking her head at his stubborn refusal to accept Garrett's innocence, Mandy entered her office and dropped into her chair. She stared at the phone. Should she call Garrett or should she give him more time? She simply didn't know what to do.

Like all law enforcement officers, Mandy understood that dealing with victims of abuse took special handling. She wasn't objective enough. She was too close to Garrett. She needed help, too.

Picking up the phone, she dialed Shari

261

Compton's number. For the first time since Mandy had known the social worker, she picked up on the first ring.

"Hello, Shari, this is Sheriff Scott. I need some information."

"About what?"

"About adult survivors of child abuse. I know someone — I just found out. What do I do?"

"If this person was willing to share that information with you, that is a huge step."

"I uncovered it on my own."

"I see. Well, many survivors feel threatened and humiliated when the abuse becomes known. Be supportive of that person's feelings. Don't pressure them to reveal things they aren't ready to talk about."

Oh, like don't accuse him of murder? Don't search his house for illegal drugs.

Mandy said, "Is it true that they have a higher risk of becoming an abuser themselves?"

"That is true, but each case is different. Most survivors suffer from terrible guilt and deep, deep anger. They feel they should have done more to protect themselves or other family members. They also have a higher risk of suicide, depression, posttraumatic stress disorder and anger management issues."

They were all things Mandy knew from her training, but it helped to have someone else reinforce her meager knowledge.

Shari said, "I'm going to fax you some information about support groups."

"That would be wonderful." Mandy knew that she and Garrett were going to need all the support they could get. If he'd allow her to help. In her mind, it was a big if.

After hanging up from her call to the social worker, Mandy tried calling Garrett. She wasn't surprised when he didn't answer, but she was disappointed and worried.

A few minutes later, Donna came in with the fax and handed it to Mandy. "Were you waiting for this list of domestic and child abuse support groups, Sheriff?"

"Thank you, Donna."

"Do we have a new case I don't know about?"

Mandy shook her head. "This is for a friend."

"I know a thing or two about domestic abuse. My first husband used to beat me when he got drunk and that was every night. My second husband was almost as bad."

"I'm so sorry, Donna. I had no idea."

"It was a long time ago. Men — who needs them? A girl is better off with a fabulous bag any day. Especially if it has money in it."

Donna turned and left, leaving Mandy to read over the letter Shari had sent. As she scanned it, she saw a name she recognized. Pastor Spencer, the man Judy had worked for, was the third name on the list.

Mandy had forgotten that he ran a shelter for abused women and their children. She circled the name. Maybe Garrett would feel more like talking to someone he'd already met rather than a stranger? Because Pastor Spencer had helped Judy get her life back on track that might carry some weight with Garrett.

After making a copy for herself, Mandy folded one page and tucked it into an envelope with Garrett's name and address on the outside. She could offer him this small amount of help, but she wanted it to be so much more.

Garrett opened his mail and found a letter from Mandy two days after the search of his property. His first reaction had been to toss it in the trash, but he didn't. He had avoided Mandy's phone calls, but that didn't keep him from thinking about her nearly every waking minute. And there had been a lot of waking minutes because he barely slept since he ordered her out of his house.

If only he could have told her in his own way. If only she hadn't seen the writing on the floor. He couldn't face the humiliation.

Mandy had circled one name in particular on the list. Judy's friend, Pastor Spencer.

Colin began crying again. The baby had been fussy for the past two days, and it was wearing on Garrett's nerves. Garrett carried the bottle he'd warmed into the living room and picked up his son.

Colin had no interest in it. He simply kept crying and trying to stuff his slobbery fist into his mouth. He didn't have a fever. All the things Garrett had learned to check didn't explain why his son kept crying.

Wiley pawed at Garrett's knee and whined, then barked sharply. Garrett pushed the dog aside.

"I don't know what he wants. Give me a break!" he shouted.

Wiley hunkered down in fright. Colin cried louder.

Guilt stabbed Garrett at the sight of Wiley's cowed expression. "I'm sorry, buddy. I didn't mean to yell."

It felt as if his control were slipping away. "Please, God, help me. Don't let me become my father." It was Garrett's worst fear.

After laying Colin back in the crib, Garrett walked into the kitchen, picked up the letter Mandy had sent and dialed Pastor Spencer's number.

THIRTEEN

As the days went by, Mandy continued to investigate J. J. and Spike's ties to the meth ring she felt certain was still operating in her area. There'd been no further reports of robberies, but Benny and Fred had arrested several teenagers for possession when they crashed a party that had gotten too loud for the neighbors.

Three of the teens had been dangerously high, but neither they nor their friends would give up the name of their dealer.

After interviewing numerous teenagers at the high school and coming up empty-handed, Mandy stopped by the main office hoping to have a word with Mr. Dobbs. If anyone had insight into who the kids were protecting it would be Cedric.

He wasn't in.

Mandy looked at his secretary in surprise. "I thought he was expecting me when I finished interviewing the kids."

"Oh, he was, but he got a call and said he had to leave. I think it was his wife. I don't think she's doing well. I do hope they get to take the cruise he's been planning for her."

"Then I guess I'll speak to him tomorrow."

"Oh, that's just it. He won't be in tomorrow. They're leaving on their cruise. Can you imagine sailing around the Bahamas? I think it's the most romantic gesture."

The secretary reached toward her phone. "Would you like to speak to our vice principal? He'll be taking over Mr. Dobbs's duties."

"No. Thank you." Mandy left the school with her mind in a whirl. A cruise was a big expense for a man who'd had to sell his house to afford his wife's cancer treatment. Mandy didn't go back to the office. Instead, she drove to the apartment complex where Cedric and his wife lived and parked across the street.

She didn't want to believe the man responsible for the education of the town's teenagers could be involved in something as deadly as selling meth, but she had to be sure. Desperate people sometimes did desperate things.

Crossing the street, she knocked on his apartment door. When he answered, she could see at once that he was nervous.

"Mr. Dobbs, can I have a word with you?"

"I'm busy right now. Can it wait?"

"No, it can't. I'm investigating some suspicious activity in this complex."

He stepped outside with her and pulled the door closed. "What kind of activity?"

"An abnormally high number of parcel deliveries are being made here."

His shoulders slumped as the breath whooshed out of him. "So you know?"

Mandy didn't know anything for certain, but she knew how to bluff. "I wanted to hear your side of the story before I did anything . . . official."

"Martha will die without these treatments. I know the drug isn't FDA-approved and therefore illegal to import from Mexico, but it's the only way I can afford it. It's helping. I know it is."

"But you can afford a cruise to the Bahamas?"

"I sold my car and the teachers at the school chipped in the rest. Martha has always wanted to go there. This is her last chance."

Mandy faced a quandary unlike anything she'd faced before. Cedric loved his wife. They had so little time left to spend together. What if it were she and Garrett?

Wouldn't she treasure each second with him? Try anything to save him?

"Please, Sheriff," Cedric pleaded. "Let me take her on this one last trip. When we get back . . . I'll turn myself in. I promise."

Mandy came to a decision. She laid a hand on his shoulder. "For what? I haven't seen anything illegal."

Tears welled up in his eyes as he gripped her hand. "Thank you. Thank you so much."

"I'm going to check out your story, but I want you to know that I'm praying for you and your wife."

He nodded, unable to speak.

Mandy left and returned to her car. As she drove back to the office, her spirits sagged lower.

She was no closer to busting her unknown meth dealer or to finding Judy's murderer. If she hadn't broken the law by letting Mr. Dobbs go then she'd bent it severely. Garrett wasn't speaking to her and she had no idea when she'd see Colin again.

Maybe Fred was right. Maybe she couldn't do this job. Maybe she should resign.

While she was considering what she should do, her phone rang. Hoping it was Garrett, she quickly answered. It was the hospital's ER physician.

"Sheriff, I've got two teenagers here suffering from severe overdoses of meth. Both kids are being helicoptered to the medical center in Wichita as we speak. At this point, it's doubtful that the young woman will survive. Her boyfriend was in serious condition, but I think he'll make it."

"I'm on my way. Can he be interviewed?"

"The chopper has already taken off, but there's something you need to know. The boy is Luke Holt."

Mandy's heart sank as she pulled into the station parking lot. Ken would be devastated when he got the news. "Thanks for letting me know. Have the families been notified?"

"Yes, both sets of parents are already on their way."

"All right. I'll have someone come by and take your statement."

Mandy hung up and rushed into the office just as Donna was on her way out. Donna took a step back. "Where are you going in such a hurry?"

"Call in one of the part-time officers to cover for me and send Fred to the hospital to take the staff's statements."

"What's going on?"

"Luke Holt and his girlfriend have been medevaced to Wichita with meth overdoses. I'm on my way to interview them. Maybe now someone will talk."

■ ■ ■ ■

When Mandy entered Luke Holt's hospital room, the boy's parents were seated beside his bed. His father rose and took a wide-legged aggressive stance in front of his son as he confronted Mandy. "Why haven't you gotten these thugs and their drugs out of Timber Wells? They could have killed my boy. Why aren't you doing your job?"

Luke's mother grasped his arm. "Nils, please."

Mandy understood his anger. He wanted to protect his son. Right now, he was feeling as if he'd failed.

Lord, I pray this broken family finds comfort in You.

"Mr. Holt, your son is the one person who can stop these people. I need to ask him a few questions."

He folded his arms across his chest and stepped away to stare out the window. Mandy withdrew her notebook and walked up to the bed. IV pumps sat on both sides of the bed. Luke's color was pale. He had an oxygen mask over his face and a heart monitor beeped softly above his head. "Luke, I need the name of the person who sold you the drugs."

The boy turned his face away. "I won't talk to the cops."

"Your girlfriend may die. By protecting the person responsible, you become an accessory."

Mrs. Holt leaned forward to stroke her son's hair. "You need to do the right thing. Tell Sheriff Scott what she needs to know."

"You don't understand, Mom. They'll hurt you or Dad or Ken. I can't —" He pressed his lips together, but Mandy saw the quiver in his chin.

She closed her notebook. "Mr. and Mrs. Holt, may I speak to Luke alone?"

The parents exchanged worried looks, but nodded in agreement. When the door closed behind them, Mandy took a seat beside the bed.

"Luke, these people can only hurt others if you allow them to go unpunished. I won't lie to you. I can't be everywhere all the time. I can't promise I can protect you and your family. What I can promise is that I'll do my level best to see that the people responsible spend a very long time in jail. But I can't do it without your help."

He was quiet for so long that she almost gave up hope. But at last, he said, "J. J. gave me the stuff to sell for him. He said he had a local supplier who could get me all I could

273

sell and more. It sounded so easy. The money they promised me was more than I ever dreamed of making. I've been high a few times. I didn't get hooked. I didn't know it would . . . kill anyone. I just wanted to have some fun."

"Do you have any idea who J. J.'s supplier is?"

"Last Friday night, I was coming back from a party in Topeka. It must have been three in the morning. I pulled in for gas at Turner's. I saw Spike and J. J. coming out of the salvage yard with a couple of boxes."

J. J. worked for Aaron Turner. Doing business at three in the morning was suspicious, but it wasn't a crime. She needed more than her dislike of the men to take before a judge. "Can you think of anything else that might tie the men together in this?"

"The next night, J. J. brought me my supply in the same kind of box. It was white with a blue globe on it."

"Where is the box now?" It could hold drug traces, fingerprints or DNA that might crack her case.

"J. J. dumped the drugs into my car trunk and tossed the box back in his tow truck."

"He was driving Turner's tow truck?"

"Yeah."

It wasn't much, but was it enough for

probable cause? Could she get a search warrant? If not, she'd have to set up surveillance on J. J. and the station, but that would take time. In the meanwhile, more kids were in danger.

"One other thing, Sheriff. J. J. was bragging that they've been cooking under your nose."

"Thanks, Luke. You've done the right thing."

"Please, don't tell my brother I was dealing."

"I won't tell Ken, but he's going to find out anyway. You need to be straight with him and with your folks."

"They're gonna hate me."

"I very much doubt that. They love you. Give them a chance to show it."

Rising, she opened the door and stepped into the hall where Mr. and Mrs. Holt were waiting.

Ken came rushing down the hall toward them. "I got here as soon as I could. How is he?"

Mandy said, "The doctors say he's serious but stable. Luke has made some mistakes. He's scared, but he's done a very brave thing today. I thought you should know that."

After leaving the family, Mandy checked

on Luke's girlfriend and learned her condition was improving. Thankful for that bit of news, Mandy left the building and headed for home. Once she was on the open highway, she pulled out her cell phone and called the office.

As soon as Donna answered, Mandy said, "I need a search warrant drawn up for the Turner salvage yard, the store and all their vehicles."

"Turner's? Why?"

"I have a witness who says their place is being used to move drugs."

"Really? How soon do you need this? We've been busy today."

"I'm two hours away. I want it ready by the time I get there. Is Fred or Benny in?"

"Um, they're both out on calls right now."

"Get hold of them and have them meet me at the office. I want to execute this warrant today."

"Is this the break you were hoping for?"

"Luke Holt is willing to testify he bought meth from J. J. and that J. J. used Turner's tow truck to deliver the stuff. Luke saw him picking up the drugs at the salvage yard."

"Wow."

"I'm going to give you all the information for the warrant request. I'm not letting these creeps get away this time."

Garrett walked out of his barn into the hot noonday sun. He didn't recognize the green van in the yard, but he did recognize the man standing beside it. Aaron Turner. What did he want?

Garrett walked toward him. "Afternoon."

Aaron smiled his slick I-know-I'm-better-than-you grin that had never sat right with Garrett. He didn't smile in return. "What can I help you with?"

Aaron turned his head in all directions. "I'm looking to buy salvage. Scrap metal is what I need. I'll take old tin, even old cars or trucks that don't run. I pay top price for it."

Garrett shook his head. "I don't have anything like that."

"No?" Aaron's smile dimmed. "Do you know who might?"

"You can check with Ina Purdy down the road."

"Great. You wouldn't happen to have a phone number for her, would you?"

"Sure. Come up to the house and I'll get it."

Garrett walked ahead of the man, impatient at the delay in getting his work done.

When he opened the door, the cold barrel of a gun pressed to his temple stopped him in midstep.

"Move into the kitchen, cowboy, but move real slow." It was Mike Peters.

Fear sent Garrett's heart racing. Had they hurt Colin? "Where's my son?"

"Sleeping like a baby. For now." The implied threat chilled Garrett more than the gun at his head.

"What do you want?"

"I want you to ask another stupid question, so I can blow a hole through you."

Garrett clenched his jaws together and walked forward with his hands raised. In the kitchen, he stopped. Wiley crept out from under the table and whined. Mike sneered at him. "Get outta here, mutt, or you'll get my boot again."

Aaron squatted and held out his hand. "It's just a dog. He's kinda cute. Don't he look like the pup we had when we was kids?"

Mike's eyes never left Garrett. "I hated that cur. He bit my leg."

"Yeah, yeah. Come here, boy," Aaron coaxed, patting his thigh.

As much as Garrett wished Wiley would morph into an attack dog, it didn't happen, but neither did he venture near Aaron. He stayed at Garrett's side.

Aaron looked at Garrett. "What's his name?"

"Wiley."

"Like the coyote." Aaron smiled. "I like that."

Mike reached out and took Garrett's cell phone from his shirt pocket. He handed it to Aaron. "Make the call, then get outside and hide the van."

With a disgruntled glare at Mike, Aaron took the phone and left.

Mike gestured with the gun toward a chair in the center of the room. "Take a seat and don't try anything stupid. Behave and your kid lives another day."

Impotent rage threatened to choke Garrett. He struggled to stay calm. He might be able to rush the man and overpower him, but if he got himself killed, there wouldn't be anyone to protect Colin.

"If you do anything to harm my son —" Garrett bit off the threat.

Mike walked behind Garrett and shoved him down into the chair. "Didn't I make myself clear? *You* are the one who will get him hurt. Now, shut up and get comfortable. We've got a while to wait."

Who or what were they waiting for?

Sudden blinding pain exploded through

279

Garrett's skull. He felt himself falling —
then nothing.

FOURTEEN

Mandy saw the tow truck parked beside the filling station as she drove into Timber Wells. It was hard to resist the urge to stop and search it. Nothing she found would be admissible in court without a warrant or clear probable cause. She didn't want this case thrown out on a technicality and she didn't want to spook the perpetrators into destroying evidence by showing undue interest in the place.

She slowed down as she drove by, hoping to see an obvious reason to stop, but the place was quiet.

When she turned into the department parking lot at the rear of the courthouse, she frowned. Both squad cars were gone. Why weren't Benny and Fred waiting for her?

She hurried into the building and saw Donna at the desk. "Where is everyone?"

"Fred just radioed in a bad car wreck east

of town. Benny is on his way to help."

"Fatalities?"

"I don't know. Sheriff, there's something else. I just took a call from Garrett Bowen. The man has flipped out. He's threatening to kill himself and his son."

Mandy stared at Donna in stunned disbelief. "You can't be serious. Garrett would never hurt Colin."

"All I know is what he told me."

"Are you sure it wasn't a prank? Someone claiming to be Garrett?"

"The call came from his cell-phone number. He really sounded desperate. I think he's serious."

"Who's responding?"

"I haven't given it to anyone. That's what I'm telling you. It *just* came in."

Mandy had to hear for herself that it was Garrett. "Play the tape back for me."

"I can't. The recorder has been malfunctioning since last shift. I told you we needed to replace it."

Mandy grabbed her phone and punched in Garrett's number. It rang a few times, then went to voice mail. Frustrated, she tried his home phone with the same results.

She snapped her phone shut. "Is my warrant ready?"

"Not yet. The judge was tied up in court."

"I'm going to the Bowen ranch. Get hold of the pastor at our church and tell him to meet me at Garrett's ranch as soon a possible."

"Right away."

Once she was back in the squad car, Mandy switched on her lights and siren and stepped on the gas. What had happened to drive Garrett to such despair?

Miss Compton's stories about the breakdowns suffered by adult survivors of child abuse flooded Mandy's mind. Many of them couldn't deal with the shame and guilt, but Mandy believed Garrett was strong. He had Colin to live for. He had *her* love even if he didn't know it. Was it enough?

Please, God, let it be enough.

The prayer echoed over and over in her mind until she reached the ranch. Braking to a sliding stop, she saw his truck parked beside the door. Suddenly, she realized her breath was coming in harsh, short gasps. She needed to be calm.

Garrett would need her to be calm.

Stepping out of the vehicle, she called his name and waited for an answer. None came. All she heard was the whistling of the wind past her ears and the hammering of her own heart.

Please, God, let him be okay.

She called again. "Garrett, it's Mandy. Where are you?"

Walking toward the house, she heard Colin begin crying and she rushed forward. The front door was open. Through the screen, she saw Garrett lying on the floor. A gun lay beside his outstretched hand.

"Dear God, no!" Her knees buckled and she grabbed the wall for support. The roaring in her ears drowned Colin's cries. Only her years of training kept her from crumpling to the floor.

Struggling to breathe, Mandy pulled open the screen door and rushed in.

A familiar voice behind her said, "Hold it right there, Sheriff. I don't want to shoot you if I don't have to."

Garrett heard his name being called from a long way off. He opened his eyes, but the light shot blinding pain through his skull.

He tried, but couldn't remember what he'd done to make his father so mad this time. Was his mother okay?

"Garrett, please wake up."

It was Mandy's voice pleading with him. She sounded so worried. He could hear Colin crying furiously. His son needed him. Garrett tried once more to open his eyes and succeeded in spite of the pain.

Mandy's beautiful face swam into focus. Tears stained her cheeks. His head was pillowed on her lap. After one false start, he managed to croak, "What's wrong?"

"I'm so sorry."

"He's awake, little brother," a voice called out behind him.

Garrett's memory returned in a flash and with it helpless rage.

"You're brothers?" Mandy asked in surprise. She was sitting on his kitchen floor with her back against the cabinet, holding his throbbing head. Wiley was snuggled at her side and licking Garrett's hand.

Aaron laughed. "Yeah, ain't it a hoot?"

Garrett pushed the dog away and moved to sit up beside Mandy. The effort made him gag, but he fought down the nausea and forced himself to survey the room.

Aaron, leering at Mandy, rose from where he'd been straddling a chair. Mike paced back and forth outside on the front porch.

"Are you okay?" Mandy asked Garrett quietly.

"I've been better. What are you doing here?"

"I got a call that you were threatening suicide."

"And you believed that?"

"You didn't answer the phone. I had to

come check. When I got here and saw you lying on the floor, I walked right into their trap."

"What do they want?"

Aaron raised the gun he held. "I want you to stop talking."

Mike quit pacing and shouted to Aaron, "Can't you do something about that crying brat?"

"Like what?" Aaron snapped back. "We can't get rid of him, you know that."

They weren't going to hurt Colin. Garrett sagged back against the counter. *Thank you, God.*

Looking at Mandy, he saw the same relief written on her face. He loved her so much. Why hadn't he told her?

Lord, if You get Mandy and Colin out of here, it doesn't matter what happens to me.

Calmly, Garrett said, "He's hungry. There's a bottle for him in the fridge."

Aaron backed toward the refrigerator, his gun still trained on them. He opened the door and pulled out Colin's bottle. Wiley, who'd been sitting quietly beside Garrett, padded over to sit in front of Aaron. "Sorry, pup, I got nothing for you."

Sidestepping away, he held out the bottle toward Mike. "Give him this."

Coming in through the door, Mike

stopped short. "Are you crazy? You're leaving your prints all over the place." Wiley scampered under the table at the harsh sound of his voice.

Pulling a red shop rag from his hip pocket, Mike wrapped it around the bottle and carried it into the other room.

"Giving it to him cold will make him sick," Garrett said, praying the men would find compassion in their hearts for his son.

Aaron's smile sent shivers crawling down Garrett's spine. "If it gives that witch's brat a bellyache, that's fine with me. If she hadn't recognized Mike that morning, none of this would have happened."

Icy coldness settled in Garrett's blood. "You killed Judy?"

"I heard you killed her." Aaron smirked, dividing his attention between watching them and checking on his brother's activity in the living room. A few seconds later, Colin quieted and Mike brushed past Aaron as he walked back out on the porch.

"If it's a hostage you want, take me and let Garrett and the baby go," Mandy said quickly,

Garrett cringed in fear for her. He took hold of her arm to silence her.

"I said no talking." Aaron walked back toward her, brandishing the gun.

"You're going to kill me anyway."

"True, but I'd rather not do it yet."

"The suicide call was a clever way to get me here. Was it your idea?"

"Somebody else came up with that one." He chuckled to himself.

Mandy sat back with a quick gasp. "How could I have been so blind?"

It was clear she had figured something out, but Garrett didn't have a clue. He heard a car approaching. Aaron glanced toward the door, then back at them. "Looks like the gang's all here."

Outside, a car door slammed. Garrett caught the sound of heavy boots on the steps and a glimpse of a blue uniform through the door. His surge of hope was cut short when Donna Clareborn walked into the house.

Aaron wagged his brows at Garrett. "Say hello to Mom."

Donna's smug smile made Mandy sick to her stomach. "Hello, Sheriff. I see you've met my stepsons."

All the pieces had fallen into place for Mandy, but not soon enough. It was a mistake that would cost her her life. Shaking her head in disbelief, Mandy asked, "Donna, why are you doing this?"

"I *was* making a lot of money until you started interfering." She tapped Aaron's arm. "Give me the gun and go help your brother."

"Yes, Mommy." Aaron flashed a wide grin at Mandy and laughed as he went out the door.

Mandy needed time to think of a way out. She decided to keep Donna talking as long as possible. "You always wanted to know where your people were. I've got to hand it to you. You had me fooled."

A cold, calculating smile curved Donna's lips. "What better way to make sure my stepsons stay safe than to know where the police are all day long? Don't feel bad, Mandy. They didn't figure it out in the last two towns we worked in, either."

"Why meth?"

"Cheap, easy to make if you have the right stuff and very, very lucrative."

"Your TV shopping was just a cover to get ephedrine shipped right to your door." Mandy couldn't believe she'd been so blind. She'd trusted this woman.

"The Internet is a wonderful invention," Donna said. "A few clicks and a dozen boxes of cold medicine are on their way to me or the boys from Mexico. And, of course, a new handbag or two. I really do love bags and shoes, but I knew as soon as I saw you talking to my delivery man that you'd figure it out. You're such a little bulldog. It's too bad that fool of a truck driver didn't get rid of you the way I wanted. If he had, Mr. Bowen wouldn't have to die, too."

"Why implicate me?" Garrett demanded.

"It was just another red herring for our diligent sheriff. As long as she was looking for small cooking spots in outlying areas, she wouldn't be looking for a big one."

Mandy felt like such a fool. "The salvage yard."

Donna grinned maliciously. "That's right. Gas line additive, batteries, propane, all things the boys use in the business right in one spot. You didn't know we have a refrigerated truck inside the garage to store our finished product, did you? We've got a delivery system of drivers headed to all parts of the country, even our contaminated trash gets shipped out inside chopped-up cars with no one the wiser."

Mandy closed her eyes and dropped her head. "All you needed was the anhydrous ammonia. No wonder the thefts always took place when we were busy elsewhere."

"Finally, she's getting smart. By next year, my industrious boys will be expanding their business. They're going to start selling fertilizer, too. Well, some of it." She chuckled and Mandy knew then how insane she was.

"Even if you silence me, Fred will figure out what you've been doing."

"You aren't going to get away with this," Garrett added.

"Oh, but we are. Fred and Benny are out at another meth lab explosion as we speak. I'm sorry, Mandy, but the judge and the pastor never got your messages. No one knows you're here."

"You're forgetting the kids you put in the hospital. Ken's brother will testify that he bought the meth from J. J."

Donna pressed her hand to her chest. "Oh, poor J. J. Didn't I mention he died in the explosion that Fred and Benny are investigating now? It turns out that J. J. was actually cooking meth for Mr. Bowen. Spike will testify to that for immunity, plus a few thousand dollars in cash that I've put away for him."

Mandy's fingers clenched into fists. Under the table, Wiley whined, sensing the tension in the air.

Tsking and shaking her head, Donna said, "It's too bad you rushed out here to confront Bowen without waiting for backup after you were tipped off. Of course, everyone knows how concerned about that baby you are. You died a hero — just like your father, but at least you got off a shot and killed Garrett before you died."

Mandy racked her mind for a way out. She couldn't let Garrett die because of her stupidity.

Donna's gaze darted to the door. "What's taking them so long? They should be done by now." She stepped to the doorway to look out.

Mandy made eye contact with Garrett. She needed to make a move before the men returned. She read the indecision and fear on his face.

She mouthed the words, *Do you trust me?*

His lips tightened, but he nodded.

Mandy started to rise. If she could just get into a position to leap.

The movement drew Donna's attention and she swung the gun back toward Mandy. "Ah, ah, ah. You know the procedure. Sit with your feet out in front of you and your hands on your head. Behave or that precious little baby will have a terrible accident."

Mandy sank back. She'd missed her chance and now Garrett and Colin would pay the ultimate price. "No one will believe this."

"Yes, they will. I know how to stage a

crime scene. I've been to a dozen seminars on forensic procedures. Why do you think you aren't tied up? Ligature marks would be a dead giveaway. Did you know that duct tape leaves residue traces and can even hold fingerprints?"

Clearly delighted with her cunning plan, Donna continued, "My boys have hidden a stash of drugs in Garrett's cattle trailer. We'll leave a few thousand dollars somewhere where it can be found without much effort. Fred Lindholm will see exactly what I want him to see. Plus, he'll finally get to be sheriff."

"Is Fred in on this with you?"

"No, but he doesn't look beyond the obvious."

The screen door opened and Mike stepped inside. "The stuff's planted."

She handed him the gun. "Wait until I've been gone for twenty minutes and do it the way I told you. It has to look like they shot each other. I need to get back to work. I told Benny my errand would take only an hour. I'm cutting it close."

"I'll take care of things, Ma."

"I know I can count on you, honey. Make sure you wipe this place down real good." She rose on tiptoe to kiss his cheek, then turned and left. After a few moments,

Mandy heard the sound of her car driving away.

Two instead of three, the odds were getting better, except that the brothers still had guns. Mandy bit down on the inside of her cheek. When her chance came she had to be ready.

Please, God, give me the chance to save Garrett and his son.

Aaron came through the door with a plastic bag full of cash in his gloved hand. "Where do you want this?"

"Hide it upstairs somewhere."

Aaron gave the captives a wide berth and opened the stairwell door. Mandy heard him climb the steps, then his footsteps sounded overhead.

Mike wagged the gun toward the front door. "Okay, move. One false step and we kill the brat. Understood?"

Mandy glanced at Garrett. His face had drained of color, but the resolve in his eyes told her what she needed to know. He trusted her. She wouldn't let him down.

They both rose to their feet and walked slowly toward the door. As they drew level with Mike, he took a step back and closer to the table.

Mandy looked down at Wiley. "Guess we'll miss — *lunch.*"

The dog exploded from beneath the table, barking furiously and jumping in circles. Mike swung his gun toward the animal.

Mandy launched herself into Mike's midsection, carrying him backward. He fired, but the shot went wild as they fell to the floor.

She latched on to his wrist to keep him from swinging the barrel toward her. For a second, it seemed as if she had the upper hand, but he was too strong.

Rolling over, he came up on top of her. Her grip on his wrist began slipping as the barrel moved closer to her face. She summoned all her strength to hold on.

Suddenly Garrett's fist connected with Mike's face in a satisfying thud. Her attacker went limp and slumped sideways.

Mandy could hear Aaron yelling for his brother over her own harsh breathing and hammering pulse. His footsteps pounded across the ceiling. She wriggled out from under Mike's deadweight and came up with the gun. She aimed toward the stairwell door, but Garrett was in her way.

She shouted, "Move!"

Aaron burst through the door and straight into Garrett's well-placed right cross. Aaron went down and stayed down. Garrett stood over him, breathing harshly. "Never threaten my family!"

Mandy took one second to close her eyes and draw a deep breath of relief. Then she pulled her handcuffs from her belt and got to work securing Mike's hands behind his back. When she was finished, she looked at Garrett. "I've only got one set of cuffs."

Walking to the front door, Garrett pulled Wiley's leash off a hook and returned. Dropping one knee into the middle of Aaron's back, he paid no attention to the man's grunt of pain as he wrapped the nylon strapping around his wrists and pulled them tight. "This will leave a ligature mark. Hope you don't mind."

When he was finished, Garrett strode across the room and scooped Mandy into a fierce hug. "Are you okay? I was so scared for you."

"I'm fine." She allowed herself to relax for a moment inside his strong embrace.

Pushing back, she gazed up into his dark eyes so full of love that her heart stuttered. Tenderly, he caressed her face. "I love you, Mandy."

"Oh, Garrett, I love you, too. I'd like to repeat that a thousand more times, but I need to get hold of Benny. Donna has to be stopped."

Garrett nodded and stepped away. "She'll

be monitoring all the calls coming in."

"I've got his cell number. He's not going to believe this."

"He will when you bring these two in."

Mandy motioned to their captives to get to their feet. "I'm really looking forward to this family reunion."

EPILOGUE

The arrest of Donna and her stepsons was the talk of the town for several weeks, but eventually, the buzz died down and Timber Wells returned to a quiet normalcy. Mandy knew that would change as soon as the actual trial began.

When the doorbell rang on Monday evening, Mandy bolted off her mother's sofa. "I'll get it."

She'd waited all day with eager anticipation for the start of the Bible study group because Garrett was coming tonight. Every day, all day, the thought of seeing him left her giddy with happiness.

"Thank you, dear," Kathryn called after her. Mandy heard the mirth in her mother's voice. Mandy glanced back to see an amused and knowing twinkle in her mother's eyes.

At the door, Mandy inhaled sharply and blew out slowly to calm her racing heart. It didn't help. She was head over heels in the love with the man. That he was willing to seek God's word warmed her heart on the deepest level.

Knowing how much pain Garrett had endured in his life made her all the more determined to help him find the Lord's comfort.

She opened the door, a beaming smile of welcome on her face. It wasn't Garrett. It was her mother's friend Candice.

Mandy's eagerness deflated, but she kept the smile. "Hello, I'm so glad you could make it."

Extending a relish tray of assorted vegetables covered with plastic wrap, the woman said, "I brought a little something to munch on."

Mandy took the dish from her hands. "That's very kind of you."

"It's no trouble. I made one up to take by the Dobbs's place. Did you hear? Cedric's wife passed away last night?"

Mandy stepped back. "Yes, I heard that. Please come in. I'll put this in the kitchen. My mother is in the living room. Take a seat anywhere."

After Candice, Mandy moved to close the door, but made a quick check of the street first. Garrett was nowhere in sight.

But he was coming. She put her trust in his word.

She checked the clock on the wall as she unwrapped the relish dish and set it in the center of the table. Ken and Fred, both enjoying a cup of coffee, were sitting there waiting for the group to get started. Their long faces told Mandy what they'd been discussing.

Judy Bowen's murder had been solved. The meth operation had been shut down. Donna and her sons were behind bars. It should have felt good, but it didn't.

They had been betrayed by one of their own.

Ken tipped his head back to stare at the ceiling, then said, "I still can't believe Donna set us up like that."

Mandy nodded. "The thing I find hardest to believe is that a mother would not only allow, but encourage, her children to become criminals."

Fred said, "You have to admit it was a slick setup. As a dispatcher, she always knew where we were and could make sure her stepsons could move freely in the county."

Mandy nodded. "It was a perfect system until Judy Bowen recognized Mike as the drug dealer who killed her friend."

Fred shifted in his chair. "I played into

their hands a dozen times over."

Ken looked down and shook his head. "I thought Donna really cared about kids like my little brother. Instead, she used her volunteer time at school to locate vulnerable kids who were willing to try drugs. At least Luke and his girlfriend have both made a full recovery. We can be thankful for that."

Mandy moved to the sink to wash her hands. "Donna and her crew got greedy. If they had stuck to the plan of cooking meth and shipping it out of here instead of selling it locally, we might never have caught them."

"You would have eventually," Fred said.

Mandy appreciated the compliment, but gave credit where it was due. "If it hadn't been for Wiley, they would have pinned it all on Garrett and he and I would both be dead."

Mandy bit the inside of her lip. She'd come so close to losing him. The memory of seeing Garrett sprawled on the floor — thinking the worst — it would give her nightmares for years to come.

"Trust me, I've already bought Wiley a steak dinner," Garrett said from the doorway.

Mandy's heart jumped into overdrive. It had been a near thing, but thanks to God's mercy and a mutt with a food obsession, everything had worked out.

Kathryn poked her head into the kitchen. She had Colin in her arms and a bright smile on her face. "I think we're ready to get started."

Garrett reached for his son. "If you don't mind, I'm going to feed him first."

"I can do it," Kathryn offered brightly.

"I'd rather."

"All right." Kathryn handed Colin over, but there was a bright twinkle in her eyes. "Ken, Fred, would you come with me, please?"

Taking the baby, Garrett stepped aside as the men left the room. He strolled toward Mandy. Colin gurgled happily displaying the new bottom tooth he'd cut.

Looking down at Colin, Garrett said. "Son, did you say something?"

Leaning closer as if listening to what his son was telling him, Garrett said, "Maybe you should ask her yourself."

Mandy was totally in love with the man, but she wondered if she'd ever get used to this new, playful side of him.

His visits with Pastor Spencer were helping him cope with his past and overcome his lingering guilt. Garrett had found healing by helping the children at the shelter.

Once a week, he and Pastor Spencer brought a group of the inner-city kids to Timber Wells to experience ranch life. Bottle-feeding Joey had become a big attraction for the boys and girls who'd never seen a cow up close.

Walking to where Mandy stood at the sink, Garrett held his son out toward her. "Colin has something he wants to ask you."

Mandy took the baby.

"Go ahead, buddy. Give her the message." Garrett smiled his deep warm smile. The one that curled her toes and made her want to kiss him.

Willing to go along with Garrett's foolishness, Mandy looked down at Colin. Around his neck was a white bib with red printing. It said, *Will you be my mommy?*

Next to the question mark a diamond ring was pinned to the cloth.

Mandy's jaw dropped open. Delight shot through her veins. She reached for Garrett as tears of joy stung her eyes. He came into her embrace with happiness etched in every feature.

Pulling him close, she whispered in his ear, "Yes, as long as his father is part of the deal."

Garrett whispered back, "I love you, and I thank God every day for bringing both you and Colin into my life."

"I love you, too. So much." Mandy thought her heart might explode with happiness.

Colin cooed happily as he chewed his fist, but neither adult noticed. They were too busy kissing each other.

Dear Reader,

I hope you enjoyed *Speed Trap.* I wanted to take a moment to thank many of the people who helped me research this story. First off, I'd like to thank Madelon and Lowell for making me so welcome when I visited the town of Council Grove, Kansas, my inspiration for Timber Wells. They treated me better than royalty — they treated me like family.

Council Grove is a wonderfully historic town overflowing with kind and generous people. If you're ever traveling through Kansas, be sure to stop in. I'd also like to thank the sheriff and police chief who kindly allowed me to visit their offices and ask a million questions. Everyone on their staff was wonderful to me. I make no claims to procedural accuracy in *Speed Trap.* I'm a fiction writer, not a law enforcement professional. I've never even been arrested. Any mistakes in the story are my own.

By the way, the very sweet woman who works as a dispatcher there in no way influenced my choice of villains. I had that idea before I met her.

May the Lord bless and keep everyone in Council Grove and all those of you who are reading this letter.

Yours in Christ,
Patricia Davids

QUESTIONS FOR DISCUSSION

1. Mandy allowed previous experiences to color her perception of Garrett's ability to be a parent. Was it fair of her to do so?

2. Garrett hid the emotional scars of his upbringing by keeping the closet locked. How do we hide our own emotional scars? How does our faith help us cope with a painful life?

3. How was Colin a catalyst for change in both Garrett's and Mandy's lives?

4. It is never fully explained why Judy didn't tell Garrett he had a son. Why do you feel she kept silent?

5. Mandy was worried Social Services would not adequately investigate Garrett during the home visit. Was her concern justified?

6. The media often reports stories about the failure of child welfare organizations. What can we do to make sure children are protected?

7. Mandy felt her career in law enforcement had hindered her ability to be a spouse and a parent. Do you feel that is true of many law enforcement officials?

8. Why was it hard for Mandy to admit she was falling for Garrett?

9. Garrett found it hard to envision God as a loving father because his own father had been abusive. What changed his mind?

10. When Garrett and Mandy worked together to save a sick calf, how did that change their relationship?

11. Ina was portrayed as a crusty old rancher, but what was her real role in this story?

12. Garrett withdrew from Mandy when she discovered his painful secret. Why do you think he did so when he'd been on the verge of telling her himself?

13. When evidence pointed toward Garrett's involvement in the drug ring, Mandy didn't believe it. She had faith in his innocence. Have you or someone you know been put into a similar position? Was your faith in them justified?

14. Donna had been a trusted member of Mandy's team for months, which made her betrayal of them all the more painful. Has someone you trusted betrayed that trust? How did you deal with the situation?

15. Ken's younger brother had become involved with drugs. Drugs and alcohol abuse are epidemic in our society. How does our faith equip us to deal with these issues?

ABOUT THE AUTHOR

Patricia Davids continues to work as a part-time nurse in the NICU while writing full-time. She enjoys researching new stories, traveling to new locations and meeting fans along the way. She and her husband of thirty-two years live in Wichita, Kansas, along with the newest addition to the household, a stray cat named Spooky. Pat always enjoys hearing from her readers. You can contact her by mail at P.O. Box 16714, Wichita, Kansas 67216, or visit her on the Web at www.patriciadavids.com.